"I was thinking about you," David said.

Protectively, Callie's hand clutched her robe. "Me? Why?"

He shook his head. "You'll never know how much you mean to me, Callie. All you've done for us here. You're like a breath of spring after a long winter." A wry grin tugged at the corners of his mouth. "Pretty poetic for the middle of the night, huh?"

She couldn't speak. She struggled to keep her eyes from widening any more than they already had. "But that's why you hired me. To help your daughter."

"But you've done more than that." He reached across the table and laid his hand on hers. "You've helped me, too. I feel alive again, like a man released from prison, his life restored."

Callie looked at his hand pressing against the back of hers. Though her initial thought was to recoil, she enjoyed the warm pressure against her skin. She wanted to touch his unshaven cheeks with her palms. Everything in her cried out to tell him her own secret, but she pushed the urge deep inside her, praying this time the pangs would stay there.

GAIL GAYMER MARTIN

lives in Lathrup Village, Michigan, with her husband, Bob, a great supporter and proofreader. Raised in a Christian family, she wrote poetry and Nancy Drew type mysteries as a child, but only pursued publication after retiring from her career as a high school English teacher and later a professional licensed counselor. Those experiences help Gail portray real emotion in her stories. Her first novel was published in 1998.

Besides writing novels, Gail is a freelance writer with many worship resource books in publication. She is presently an adjunct instructor of English at Detroit College of Business and is involved in various church programs. When she has time, Gail sings with her church choir and is a member of Detroit Lutheran Singers in metropolitan Detroit, and she and Bob love to travel. "God has blessed my life fully," she says.

Gail loves to hear from her readers. You may write to her at: P.O. Box 760063, Lathrup Village, MI, 48076-0063.

Upon a Midnight Clear
Gail Gaymer Martin

Love Inspired®

Published by Steeple Hill Books™

STEEPLE HILL BOOKS

Steeple
Hill™

ISBN 0-373-87123-6

UPON A MIDNIGHT CLEAR

Visit us at www.steeplehill.com

Printed in U.S.A.

Then you will call upon me and come and pray to me, and I will listen to you. And you will seek me and find me, when you seek me with all your heart.

—*Jeremiah* 29:12-13

Dedicated to my sister, Jan,
who knows the sorrow of losing a child.
And in loving memory of her infant daughters,
Lisa Marie and Beth Ann, who live with Jesus.

Thanks to my husband, Bob, for his devotion,
support and hours of proofreading. To Flo Stano for
her nursing expertise, and to the Bedford Chamber
of Commerce for their invaluable information.

Chapter One

Callie Randolph scanned the employment ads of the *Indianapolis News*. Her eyes lit upon a Help Wanted entry: *Special child, aged five, needs professional caregiver. Live-in. Good wage. Contact David Hamilton. 812 area code.* Southern Indiana, she assumed. "Live-in," she wanted. But a child?

She raised her head from the ad and caught her mother, eyeing her.

"You've been quiet since you got home," Grace Randolph said, resting back in the kitchen chair. "Tell me about the funeral."

"It was nice, as funerals go. But sad, so close to the holidays." Ethel's death, coming as it did on the footsteps of Christmas, jolted Callie with the memories of a birth six Christmases earlier. Pushing away the invading thoughts, Callie shifted in her chair and focused on her mother. "More people than I would expect at the funeral for someone in her nineties, but I suppose most of the mourners were friends and business acquaintances of Ethel's children. The family has a name in the community."

"Ah yes, when we're old, people forget."

"No, it's not that they forget. When we're *that* old, many of our own friends and acquaintances have already died. Makes coming to a funeral difficult." Callie hoped to lighten Grace's negative mood. "It'll feel strange not taking care of Ethel. She had the faith of a saint and a smile right to the end. Always had a kind word." She raised her eyes, hoping her mother had heard her last statement.

Grace stared across the room as if lost in thought, and Callie's mind drifted to the funeral and the preacher's comforting words. *"Ethel lived a full and glorious life, loving her Lord and her family."* Callie pictured the wrinkled, loving face of her dying patient. Ethel's earthly years had definitely been full and glorious.

In contrast, Callie's nearly twenty-six years had been empty and dull. Her dreams had died that horrible March day that she tried to block from her memory. Her life seemed buried in its own tomb of guilt and sorrow.

"So, about the funeral—?"

Callie slammed the door on her thoughts and focused on her mother.

"Tell me about the music? Any hymns?" Grace asked.

Callie eyed her, sensing an ulterior motive in her question. "Real nice, Mom. Organ music and hymns."

"Which hymns?"

Callie pulled her shoulders back, feeling the muscles tightening along the cords of her neck. "'Amazing Grace,' 'Softly and Tenderly.'"

"I can hear you singing that one. So beautiful."

Callie fought the desire to bolt from the room. She sensed an argument heading her way. Instead, she aimed her eyes at the newspaper clutched in her hands.

Grace leaned on an elbow. "So what will you do now?"

"Find a new job, I suppose." She hesitated, wondering what comment she'd receive about her newest resolve. "But I've made a decision." Callie met her mother's eyes. "I'm not going to give elderly care anymore. I'll find something else."

"Praise the Lord, you've come to your senses. Callie, you have a nursing degree, but you continue to waste your time with the deathwatch. You need to live and use the talent God gave you."

Deep creases furrowed Callie's forehead. "Please don't call it the deathwatch. Caring for older people has been a blessing. And I *do* use my talents." She shook her head, amazed at her mother's attitude. "Do you think it's easy to nurse someone who's dying? I use as many skills as I would in a regular hospital."

Grace fell back against the chair. "I'm sorry. I don't mean to belittle your work, but it's not a life for a young woman. Look at you. You're beautiful and intelligent, yet you spend your life sitting in silent rooms, listening to old people muttering away about nothing but useless memories. What about a husband...and children? Don't you want a life for yourself?"

She flinched at her mother's words. "Please, don't

get on that topic, Mom. You know how I feel about that."

"I wish I knew when you got these odd ideas. They helped put your father in his grave. He had such hopes for you."

Callie stiffened as icy tendrils slithered through her. How many times was she reminded of how she had helped kill her father? After his death three years earlier, the doctor had said her dad had been a walking time bomb from fatty foods, cigarettes and a type-A personality. Though guilt poked at her, she knew she hadn't caused his death. Yet, she let her mother rile her.

Grace scowled with a piercing squint. "I think it began when you stopped singing," she said, releasing a lengthy, audible sigh. "Such a beautiful voice. Like a meadowlark."

"Stop. Stop, Mother." Callie slammed her hand on the tabletop. "Please, don't call me that."

Grace looked taken aback. "Well, I'm sorry. What's gotten into you?" She gaped at Callie. "You're as white as a sheet. I only called you a—"

"Please, don't say it again, Mother." Callie pressed her forehead into her hand.

"I don't know what's wrong with you." Grace sat for a moment before she began her litany. "I don't know, Callie. I could cry when I think of it. Everyone said you sang like an angel."

Callie stared at the newspaper, the black letters blurring. Her mother wouldn't stop until she'd made her point. Callie ached inside when she thought about the music she'd always loved. She struggled to keep her voice calm and controlled. "I lost my interest in music, that's all." Her fingernails dug into the flesh of her fisted hand.

"Your father had such hopes for you. He dreamed you'd pass your audition with the Jim McKee Singers. But his hopes were buried along with him in his grave."

Callie modulated her pitch, and her words came out in a monotone. "I didn't pass the audition. I told you."

"I can't believe that, Callie. You've said it, but everyone knew you could pass the audition. Either you didn't try or...I don't know. Being part of Paul Ivory's ministry would be any girl's dream. And the Jim McKee Singers traveled with him in the summer all over the country, so it wouldn't have interfered with your college studies. And then you just quit singing. I can't understand you."

"Mother, let's not argue about something that happened years ago."

"But it's not just that, Callie. I hate to bring it up, but since the baby, you've never been the same."

Unexpected tears welled in Callie's eyes, tears she usually fought. But today they sneaked in behind the emotions elicited by Ethel's death, and the memory of the baby's Christmas birth dragged them out of hiding.

Callie had never seen the daughter she bore six years earlier. The hospital had their unbending policy, and her parents had given her the same ultimatum. A girl placing a child for adoption should not see her baby.

She begged and pleaded with her parents to allow her to keep her daughter. But they would have no part of it. She struggled in her thoughts—longing to finish an argument that held weight. In the end, her parents were correct. A child needed a secure and loving home. Adoption was best for her baby daughter. But not for Callie. Against her wishes, Callie signed the papers releasing her baby for adoption.

Grace breathed a ragged sigh. "Maybe your father and I made a mistake. You were so young, a whole lifetime ahead of you. We thought you could get on with your life. If you'd only told us who the young man was—but you protected him. Any decent young man would have stood up and accepted his responsibilities. For all we knew, you never told him, either."

"We've gone over this before. It's in the past. It's over. It's too late." She clutched the newspaper, crumpling the paper beneath her fingers.

"We meant well. Even your brother and sister begged you to tell us who the fellow was. You could have been married, at least. Given the baby a name, so we could hold our head up in public. But, no."

Callie folded the paper and clasped it in her trembling hand. She rose without comment. What could she say that she hadn't said a million times already? "I'm going to my room. I have a headache." As she passed through the doorway, she glanced over her shoulder and saw her mother's strained expression.

Before Grace could call after her, Callie rushed up the staircase to her second-floor bedroom and locked the door. She could no longer bear to hear her mother's sad-voiced recollections. No one but Callie knew the true story. She prayed that the vivid picture, too much like a horror movie, would leave her. Yet so many nights the ugly dream tore into her sleep, and again and again she relived the life-changing moments.

She plopped on the corner of the bed, massaging her neck. The newspaper ad appeared in her mind. *David Hamilton.* She grabbed a pen from her desk, reread the words, and jotted his name and telephone number on a scratch pad. She'd check with Christian Care Services tomorrow and see what they had available. At least she'd have the number handy if she wanted to give Mr. Hamilton a call later.

She tossed the pad on her dressing table and stretched out on the bed. A child? The thoughts of caring for a child frightened her. Would a child, especially a sick child, stir her longing?

She'd resolved to make a change in her life. Images of caring for adults marched through her head—the thought no longer appealed to her. Nursing in a doctor's office or hospital held no interest for her: patients coming and going, a nurse with no involvement in their lives. She wanted to be part of a life, to make a difference.

She rolled on her side, dragging her fingers through the old-fashioned chenille spread. The room looked so much the way it had when she was a teenager. How long had her mother owned the antiquated bedspread?

Since college, her parents' home had been only a stop-off place between jobs. Live-in care was her preference—away from her parents' guarded eyes, as they tried to cover their sorrow and shame over all that had happened.

When she'd graduated from college, she had

weighed all the issues. Geriatric care seemed to encompass all her aspirations. At that time, she could never have considered child care. Her wounds were too fresh.

Her gaze drifted to the telephone. The name *David Hamilton* entered her mind again. Looking at her wristwatch, she wondered if it was too late to call him. Eight in the evening seemed early enough. Curiosity galloped through her mind. What did the ad mean—a "special" child? Was the little one mentally or physically challenged? A boy or girl? Where did the family live? Questions spun in her head. What would calling hurt? She'd at least have her questions answered.

She swung her legs over the edge of the bed, rose, and grabbed the notepad. What specific information would she like to know? She organized her thoughts, then punched in the long-distance number.

A rich baritone voice filled the line, and when Callie heard his commanding tone, she caught her breath. Job interviews and query telephone calls had never bothered her. Tonight her wavering emotions addled her. She drew in a lengthy, relaxing breath, then introduced herself and stated her business.

Hamilton's self-assured manner caught her off guard. "I'm looking for a professional, Ms. Randolph. What is your background?"

His tone intimidated her, and her responses to his questions sounded reticent in her ears. "It's *Miss* Randolph, and I'm a professional, licensed nurse." She paused to steady her nerves. "But I've preferred to work as a home caregiver rather than in a hospital.

The past four years, I've had elderly patients, but I'm looking for a change."

"Change?"

His abruptness struck her as arrogant, and Callie could almost sense his arched eyebrow.

"Yes. I've been blessed working with the older patients, but I'd like to work with...a child."

"I see." A thoughtful silence hung in the air. "You're a religious woman, Miss Randolph?"

His question confounded her. Then she remembered she'd used the word *blessed*. Not sure what he expected, she answered honestly. "I'm a Christian, if that's what you're asking."

She waited for a response. Yet only silence filled the line. With no response forthcoming, she asked, "What do you mean by 'special,' Mr. Hamilton? In the ad, you mentioned you needed a caregiver for a 'special child.'"

He hesitated only a moment. "Natalie...Nattie's a bright child. She was always active, delightful—but since her mother's death two years ago, she's become...withdrawn." His voice faded.

"Withdrawn?"

"Difficult to explain in words. I'd rather the prospective caregiver meet her and see for herself what I mean. Nattie no longer speaks. She barely relates to anyone. She lives in her own world."

Callie's heart lurched at the thought of a child bearing such grief. "I see. I understand why you're worried." Still, panic crept over her like cold fingers inching along her spine. Her heart already ached for the child. Could she control her own feelings? Her mind spun with flashing red warning lights.

"I've scared you off, Miss Randolph." Apprehension resounded in his statement.

She cringed, then lied a little. "No, no. I was thinking."

"Thinking?" His tone softened. "I've been looking for someone for some time now, and I seem to scare people off with the facts...the details of Nattie's problem."

The image of a lonely, motherless child tugged at her compassion. What grief he had to bear. "I'm not frightened of the facts," Callie said, but in her heart, she was frightened of herself. "I have some personal concerns that came to mind." She fumbled for what to say next. "For example, I don't know where you live. Where are you located, sir?"

"We live in Bedford, not too far from Bloomington."

Bedford. The town was only a couple of hours from her mother's house. She paused a moment. "I have some personal matters I need to consider. I'll call you as soon as I know whether I'd like to be interviewed for the position. I hope that's okay with you."

"Certainly. That's fine. I understand." Discouragement sounded in his voice.

She bit the corner of her lip. "Thank you for your time."

After she hung up the telephone, Callie sat for a while without moving. She should have been honest. She'd already made her decision. A position like that wouldn't be wise at all. She was too vulnerable.

Besides, she wasn't sure she wanted to work for David Hamilton. His tone seemed stiff and arrogant. A child needed a warm, loving father, not one who was bitter and inflexible. She would have no patience with a man like that.

David Hamilton leaned back in his chair, his hand still clasping the telephone. *Useless.* In two months, his ad had resulted in only three telephone calls. One courageous soul came for an interview, but with her first look at Nattie, David saw the answer in the woman's eyes.

He supposed, as well, the "live-in" situation might be an obstacle for some. With no response locally, he'd extended his ad further away, as far as Indianapolis. But this Miss Randolph had been the only call so far.

He longed for another housekeeper like Miriam. Her overdue retirement left a hole nearly as big, though not as horrendous, as Sara's death. No one could replace Miriam.

A shudder filtered through him. *No one could replace Sara.*

Nothing seemed worse than a wife's death, but when it happened, he had learned the truth. Worse was a child losing her mother. Yet the elderly housekeeper had stepped in with all her love and wisdom and taken charge of the household, wrapping each of them in her motherly arms.

Remembering Miriam's expert care, David preferred to hire a more mature woman as a nanny. The voice he heard on the telephone tonight sounded too young, perhaps nearly a child herself. He mentally calculated her age. She'd mentioned working for four years. If she'd graduated from college when she was twenty-one, she'd be only twenty-five. What would a twenty-five-year-old know about healing his child? Despite his despair, he felt a pitying grin flicker on his lips. He was only thirty-two. What did he know about healing his child? Nothing.

David rose from the floral-print sofa and wandered to the fireplace. He stared into the dying embers. Photographs lined the mantel, memories of happier times—Sara smiling warmly with sprinkles of sunlight and shadow in her golden hair; Nattie with her heavenly blue eyes and bright smile posed in the gnarled peach tree on the hill; and then, the photograph of Sara and him on his parents' yacht.

He turned from the photographs, now like a sad monument conjuring sorrowful memories. David's gaze traversed the room, admiring the furnishings and decor. Sara's hand had left its mark everywhere in the house, but particularly in this room. Wandering to the bay window, he stood over the mahogany grand piano, his fingers caressing the rich, dark wood. How much longer would this magnificent instrument lie silent? Even at the sound of a single note, longing knifed through him.

This room was their family's favorite spot, where they had spent quiet evenings talking about their plans and dreams. He could picture Sara and Nattie stretched out on the floor piecing together one of her thick cardboard puzzles.

An empty sigh rattled through him, and he shivered with loneliness. He pulled himself from his reveries and marched back to the fireplace, grabbing the poker and jamming it into the glowing ashes. Why should he even think, let alone worry, about the young woman's phone call? He'd never hear from her again, no matter what she promised. Her voice gave the tell-tale evidence. She had no intention of calling again.

Thinking of Nattie drew him to the hallway. He followed the wide, curved staircase to the floor above. In the lengthy hallway, he stepped quietly along the thick Persian carpet. Two doors from the end, he paused and listened. The room was silent, and he pushed the door open gently, stepping inside.

A soft night-light glowed a warm pink. Natalie's slender frame lay curled under a quilt, and the rise and fall of the delicate blanket marked her deep sleep. He moved lightly across the pink carpeting and stood, looking at her buttercup hair and her flushed, rosy cheeks. His heart lurched at the sight of his child—their child, fulfilling their hopes and completing their lives.

Or what had become their incomplete and short life together.

After the telephone call, Callie's mind filled with thoughts of David Hamilton and his young daughter. Her headache pounded worse than before, and she undressed and pulled down the blankets. Though the evening was still young, she tucked her legs beneath the warm covers.

The light shone brightly, and as thoughts drifted through her head, she nodded to herself, resolute she would not consider the job in Bedford. After turning off the light, she closed her eyes, waiting for sleep.

Her subconsciousness opened, drawing her into the darkness. The images rolled into her mind like thick fog along an inky ocean. *She was in a sparse waiting room. Her pale pink blouse, buttoned to the neck, matched the flush of excitement in her cheeks. The murky shadows swirled past her eyes: images, voices, the reverberating click of a door. Fear rose within her. She tried to scream, to yell, but nothing came except black silence—*

Callie forced herself awake, her heart thundering. Perspiration ran from her hairline. She threw back the blankets and snapped on the light. Pulling her trembling legs from beneath the covers, she sat on the edge of the bed and gasped until her breathing returned to normal.

She rose on shaking legs and tiptoed into the hall to the bathroom. Though ice traveled through her veins, a clammy heat beaded on her body. Running cold tap water onto a washcloth, she covered her face and breathed in the icy dampness. *Please, Lord, release me from that terrible dream.*

She wet the cloth again and washed her face and neck, then hurried quietly back to her room, praying for a dreamless sleep.

Chapter Two

Christian Care Services filled the two-story office building on Woodward. Callie entered the lobby and took the elevator to the second floor. Usually she walked the stairs, but today she felt drained of energy.

Twenty-five minutes later, she left more discouraged than when she'd arrived. Not one live-in care situation. How could she tell the young woman she couldn't live at home, not because she didn't love her mother, but because she loved herself as much? The explanation seemed too personal and complicated.

Feeling discouraged, she trudged to her car. Live-in positions weren't very common, and she wondered how long she'd have to wait. If need be, she'd look on her own, praying that God would lead her to a position somewhere.

Standing beside her car, she searched through her shoulder bag for her keys and, with them, pulled out the slip of paper with David Hamilton's phone number. She didn't recall putting the number in her bag, and finding it gave her an uneasy feeling. She tossed the number back into her purse.

The winter air penetrated her heavy woolen coat, and she unlocked the car door and slid in. As thoughts butted through her head, she turned on the ignition and waited for the heat.

Money wasn't an immediate problem; residing with others, she'd been able to save a tidy sum. But she needed a place to live. If she stayed home, would she and her mother survive? God commanded children to honor their parents, but had God meant Callie's mother? A faint smile crossed her lips at the foolish thought. Callie knew her parents had always meant well, but meaning and reality didn't necessarily go hand in hand.

Indianapolis had a variety of hospitals. She could probably have her pick of positions in the metropolitan area, then get her own apartment or condo. But again the feeling of emptiness consumed her. She wasn't cut out for hospital nursing.

Warmth drifted from the car heater, and Callie moved the button to high. She felt chilled deep in her bones. Though the heat rose around her, icy sensations nipped at her heart. Her memory turned back to her telephone call the previous evening and to a little child who needed love and care.

She shook the thought from her head and pulled out of the parking lot. She'd give the agency a couple of weeks. If nothing became available, then she'd know Bedford was God's decision. By that time, the position might already be taken, and her dilemma would be resolved.

* * *

Callie glanced at David Hamilton's address again. Bedford was no metropolis, and she'd found the street easily.

Two weeks had passed and no live-in positions had become available, not even for an elderly patient. Her twenty-sixth birthday had plodded by a week earlier, and she felt like an old, jobless woman, staring at the girlish daisy wallpaper in her bedroom. Life had come to a standstill, going nowhere. Tired of sitting by the telephone waiting for a job call, she had called David Hamilton. Despite his lack of warmth, he had a child who needed someone to love her.

Keeping her eyes on the winding road lined with sprawling houses, she glanced at the slip of paper and reread the address. A mailbox caught her eye. The name *Hamilton* jumped from the shiny black receptacle in white letters. She looked between the fence pillars, and her gaze traveled up the winding driveway to the large home of oatmeal-colored limestone.

She aimed her car and followed the curved pathway to the house. Wide steps led to a deep, covered porch, and on one side of the home, a circular tower rose above the house topped by a conical roof.

Callie pulled in front, awed by the elegance and charm of the turn-of-the-century building. Sitting for a moment to collect her thoughts, she pressed her tired back against the seat cushion. Though an easy trip in the summer, the two-hour drive on winter roads was less than pleasant. She thanked God the highway was basically clear.

Closing her eyes, she prayed. Even thinking of Mr. Hamilton sent a shudder down her spine. His voice presented a formidable image in her mind, and now she would see him face-to-face.

She climbed from the car and made her way up the impressive steps to the wide porch. Standing on the expanse of cement, she had a closer view of the large tower rising along the side. *Like a castle,* she thought. She located the bell and pushed. Inside, a chime sounded, and she waited.

When the door swung open, she faced a plump, middle-aged woman who stared at her through the storm door. The housekeeper, Callie assumed. The woman pushed the door open slightly, giving a flicker of a smile. "Miss Randolph?"

"Yes," Callie answered.

The opening widened, and the woman stepped aside. "Mr. Hamilton is waiting for you in the family parlor. May I take your coat?"

Callie regarded her surroundings as she slid the coat from her shoulders. She stood in a wide hallway graced by a broad, curved staircase and a sparkling crystal chandelier. An oriental carpet covered the floor, stretching the length of the entry.

Two sets of double doors stood closed on the right, and on the left, three more sets of French doors hid the rooms' interiors, leaving Callie with a sense of foreboding. Were the doors holding something in? Or keeping something out? Only the door at the end of the hallway stood open, probably leading to the servants' quarters.

The woman disposed of Callie's coat and gestured for her to follow. The housekeeper moved to the left, rapped lightly on the first set of doors, and, when a muffled voice spoke, pushed the door open and stepped aside.

Callie moved forward and paused in the doorway. The room was lovely, filled with floral-print furnishings and a broad mantel displaying family photographs. Winter sunlight beamed through a wide bay window, casting French-pane patterns on the elegant mahogany grand piano. But what caught her off guard the most was the man.

David Hamilton stood before the fireplace, watching her. Their eyes met and locked in unspoken curiosity. A pair of gray woolen slacks and a burgundy sweater covered his tall, athletic frame. His broad shoulders looked like a swimmer's, and tapered to a trim waist.

He stepped toward her, extending his hand without a smile. "Miss Randolph."

She moved forward to meet him halfway. "Mr. Hamilton. You have a lovely home. Very gracious and charming."

"Thank you. Have a seat by the fire. Big, old homes sometimes hold a chill. The fireplace makes it more tolerable."

After glancing around, she made her way toward a chair near the hearth, then straightened her skirt as she eased into it. The man sat across from her, stretching his long legs toward the warmth of the fire. He was far more handsome than she had imagined, and she chided herself for creating an ogre, rather than this attractive tawny-haired man whose hazel eyes glinted sparks of green and brown as he observed her.

"So," he said. His deep, resonant voice filled the silence.

She pulled herself up straighter in the chair and acknowledged him. "I suppose you'd like to see my references?"

He sat unmoving. "Not really."

His abrupt comment threw her off balance a moment. "Oh? Then you'd like to know my qualifications?"

"No, I'd rather get to know *you*." His gaze penetrated hers, and she felt a prickling of nerves tingle up her arms and catch in her chest.

"You mean my life story? Why I became a nurse? Why I'd rather do home care?"

"Tell me about your interests. What amuses you?"

She looked directly into his eyes. "My interests? I love to read. In fact, I brought a small gift for Natalie, some children's books. I thought she might like them. I've always favored children's literature."

He stared at her with an amused grin on his lips.

"I guess I'm rattling. I'm nervous. I've cared for the elderly, but this is my first interview for a child."

David nodded. "You're not much beyond a child yourself."

Callie sat bolt upright. "I'm twenty-six, Mr. Hamilton. I believe I qualify as an adult. And I'm a registered nurse. I'm licensed to care for people of all ages."

He raised his hand, flexing his palm like a policeman halting traffic. "Whoa. I'm sorry, Miss Randolph. I didn't mean to insult you. You have a very youthful appearance. You told me your qualifications on the telephone. I know you're a nurse. If I didn't think you might be suited for this position, I wouldn't have wasted my time. Nor yours."

Callie's cheeks burned. "I'm sorry. I thought, you—"

"Don't apologize. I was abrupt. Please continue. How else do you spend your time?"

She thought for a moment. "As I said before, I love to read. I enjoy the theater. And the outdoors. I'm not interested in sports, but I enjoy a long walk on a spring morning or a hike through the woods in autumn— Do I sound boring?"

"No, not at all."

"And then I love…" She hesitated. *Music.* How could she tell him her feelings about music and singing? So much time had passed.

His eyes searched hers, and he waited.

The grandfather clock sitting across the room broke the heavy silence. *One. Two. Three.*

He glanced at his wristwatch. "And then you love…"

She glanced across the room at the silent piano. "Music."

Chapter Three

Callie waited for a comment, but David Hamilton only shifted his focus to the piano, then back to her face.

She didn't mention her singing. "I play the piano a little." She gestured toward the impressive instrument. "Do you play?"

David's face tightened, and a frown flickered on his brow. "Not really. Not anymore. Sara, my wife, played. She was the musician in the family."

Callie nodded. "I see." His eyes flooded with sorrow, and she understood. The thought of singing filled her with longing, too. They shared a similar ache, but hers was too personal, too horrible to even talk about. Her thought returned to the child. "And Natalie? Is your daughter musical?"

Grief shadowed his face again, and she was sorry she'd asked.

"I believe she is. She showed promise before her

mother died. Nattie was four then and used to sing songs with us. Now she doesn't sing a note.''

''I'm sorry. It must be difficult, losing a wife and in a sense your daughter.'' Callie drew in a deep breath. ''Someday, she'll sing again. I'm sure she will. When you love music, it has to come out. You can't keep it buried inside of…''

The truth of her words hit her. Music pushed against her heart daily. Would she ever be able to think of music without the awful memories surging through her? Her throat ached to sing, but then the black dreams rose like demons, just as Nattie's singing probably aroused sad thoughts of her mother.

David stared at her curiously, his head tilting to one side as he searched her face. She swallowed, feeling the heat of discomfort rise in her again.

''You have strong feelings about music.'' His words were not a question.

''Yes, I do. She'll sing. After her pain goes away.'' Callie's thoughts turned to a prayer. *Help me to sing again, Lord, when my hurt is gone.*

''Excuse me.'' David Hamilton rose. ''I want to see if Agnes is bringing our tea.'' He stepped toward the door, then stopped. ''Do you like tea?''

Callie nodded. ''Yes, very much.''

He turned and strode through the doorway. Callie drew in a calming breath. Why did she feel as if he were sitting in judgment of her, rather than interviewing her? She raised her eyebrows. Maybe he was.

In only a moment, David spoke to her from the parlor doorway. ''Agnes is on her way.'' He left the door open, and before he had crossed the room, the woman she'd seen earlier entered with a tray.

"Right here, Agnes. On the coffee table is fine." He gestured to the low table that stretched between them. "Miss Randolph, this is Agnes, my housekeeper. She's caring for Nattie until I find someone."

"We met at the door. It's nice to know you, Agnes." The woman nodded and set the tray on the highly polished table.

"Agnes has been a godsend for us since we lost Miriam."

"Thank you, Mr. Hamilton," she said, glancing at him. "Would you like me to pour?"

"No, I'll get it. You have plenty to do." With a flicker of emotion, his eyes rose to meet the woman's. "By the way, have you checked on Nattie lately?"

"Yes, sir, she's coloring in her room."

"Coloring? That's good. I'll take Miss Randolph up to meet her a bit later."

Agnes nodded and left the room, closing the door behind her. David poured tea into the two china cups. "I'll let you add your own cream and sugar, if you take it," he said, indicating toward the pitcher and sugar bowl on the tray. "And please have a piece of Agnes's cake. It's lemon. And wonderful."

Callie glanced at him, astounded at the sudden congeniality in his voice. The interview had felt so ponderous, but now he sounded human. "Thanks. I take my tea black. And the cake looks wonderful." She sipped the strong tea, and then placed the cup on the tray and picked up a dessert plate of cake.

David eyed her as she slivered off a bite and forked it into her mouth. The tangy lemon burst with flavor on her tongue. "It's delicious."

He looked pleased. "I will say, Agnes is an excellent cook."

"Has she been with you long?"

He stared into the red glow of the firelight. "No—a half year, perhaps. Miriam, my past housekeeper, took Nattie—took all of us—under her wing when Sara died. She had been with my parents before their deaths. A longtime employee of the family. She retired. Illness and age finally caught up with her. Her loss has been difficult for us."

He raised his eyes from the mesmerizing flames. "I'm sorry, Miss Randolph. I'm sure you aren't interested in my family tree, nor my family's problems."

"Don't apologize, please. And call me Callie." She felt her face brighten to a shy grin. "Miss Randolph sounds like my maiden aunt."

For the first time, his tense lips relaxed and curved to a pleasant smile. "All right. It's Callie," he said, leaning back in the chair. "Is that short for something?"

"No, just plain Callie."

He nodded. "So, Callie, tell me how a young woman like you decided to care for the elderly. Why not a position in a hospital, regular hours so you could have fun with your friends?"

She raised her eyes to his and fought the frown that pulled at her forehead. Never had an interview caused her such stress. The man seemed to be probing at every nerve ending—searching for what, she didn't know. She grasped for the story she had lived with for so long.

"When I graduated from college, I had romantic

dreams. Like Florence Nightingale, I suppose. A hospital didn't interest me. I wanted something more...absorbing. So I thought I'd try my hand at home care. The first job I had was a cancer patient, an elderly woman who needed constant attention. Because of that, I was asked to live in their home, which suited me nicely."

"You have no family, then?"

She swallowed. How could she explain her relationship with her mother. "Yes, my mother is living. My father died about three years ago. But my mother's in good health and active. She doesn't need me around. My siblings are older. My brother lives right outside Indianapolis. My sister and her husband live in California."

"No apartment or home of your own?"

"My mother's house is the most permanent residence I have. No, I have no other financial responsibilities, if that's what you're asking."

David grimaced. "I wasn't trying to pry. I wondered if a live-in situation meets your needs."

"Yes, but most important, I like the involvement, not only with the patient, but with the family. You know—dedication, commitment."

A sound between a snicker and harrumph escaped him. "A job here would certainly take dedication and commitment."

"That's what I want. I believe God has a purpose for everybody. I want to do something that has meaning. I want to know that I'm paying God back for—"

"Paying God back?" His brows lifted. "Like an atonement? What kind of atonement does a young woman like you have to make?"

Irritation flooded through her, and her pitch raised along with her volume. "I didn't say *atonement*, Mr. Hamilton. I said *purpose*. And you've mentioned my *young* age often since I've arrived. I assume my age bothers you."

The sensation that shot through Callie surprised even her. Why was she fighting for a job she wasn't sure she wanted? A job she wasn't sure she could handle? A sigh escaped her. Working with the child wasn't a problem. She had the skills.

But *Callie* was the problem. Already, she found herself emotionally caught in the child's plight, her own buried feelings struggling to rise from within. Her focus settled upon David Hamilton's startled face. How could she have raised her voice to this man? Even if she wanted the position, any hopes of a job here were now lost forever.

David was startled by the words of the irate young woman who stood before him. He dropped against the back of his chair, peering at her and flinching against her sudden anger. He reviewed what he'd said. Had he made a point of her age?

A flush rose to her face, and for some reason, she ruffled his curiosity. He sensed a depth in her, something that aroused him, something that dragged his own empathy from its hiding place. He'd felt sorry for himself and for Nattie for such a long time. Feeling grief for someone else seemed alien.

"To be honest, Miss Rand—Callie, I had thought to hire an older woman. Someone with experience who could nurture Nattie and bring her back to the sweet, happy child she was before her mother's death.''

Callie's chin jutted upward. Obviously his words had riled her again.

"Was your wife an old woman, Mr. Hamilton?"

A rush of heat dashed to his cheeks. "What do you mean?"

"I mean, did your wife understand your child? Did she love her? Could she relate to her? Play with her? Sing with her? Give her love and care?"

David stared at her. "Wh-why, yes. Obviously." His pulse raced and pounded in his temples, not from anger but from astonishment. She seemed to be interviewing him, and he wasn't sure he liked it, at all.

"Then why does a nanny—a caregiver—have to be an elderly woman? Can't a woman my age—perhaps your wife's age when she died—love and care for your child? I don't understand."

Neither did he understand. He stared at her and closed his gaping mouth. Her words struck him like icy water. What she said was utterly true. Who was he protecting? Nattie? Or himself? He peered into her snapping eyes. *Spunky? Nervy?* No, *spirited* was the word.

He gazed at the glowing, animated face of the woman sitting across from him. Her trim body looked rigid, and she stared at him with eyes the color of the sky or flowers. Yes, delphiniums. Her honey-colored hair framed an oval face graced with sculptured cheekbones and full lips. She had fire, soul and vigor. Isn't that what Nattie needed?

Callie's voice softened. "I'm sorry, Mr. Hamilton.

You're angry with me. I did speak to you disrespect-fully, and I'm sorry. But I—''

"No. No, I'm not angry. You've made me think. I see no reason why Nattie should have an elderly nanny. A young woman might tempt her out of her shell. She's needs to be around activity and laughter. She needs to play." He felt tears push against the back of his eyes, and he struggled. He refused to sit in front of this stranger and sob, bearing his soul like a blithering idiot. "She needs to have fun. Yes?"

"Yes." She shifted in her chair, seemingly embar-rassed. "I'm glad you agree." Callie stared into her lap a moment. "How does she spend her day now?"

"Sitting. Staring into space. Sometimes she colors, like today. But often her pictures are covered in dark brown or purple. Or black."

"No school?"

David shook his head. "No. We registered her for kindergarten, but I couldn't follow through. I took her there and forced her from the car, rigid and silent. I couldn't do that to her. But next September is first grade. She must begin school then. I could get a tutor, but..." The memories of the first school day tore at his heart.

"But that won't solve the problem."

He lifted his eyes to hers. "Yes. A tutor won't solve a single problem."

"Well, you have seven or eight months before school begins. Was she examined by doctors? I as-sume she has nothing physically wrong with her."

"She's healthy. She eats well. But she's lethargic, prefers to be alone, sits for hours staring outside, sometimes at a book. Occasionally, she says something to me—a word, perhaps. That's all.''

Callie was silent, then asked, "Psychological? Have you seen a therapist?''

"Yes, the physician brought in a psychiatrist as a consultant.'' He recalled that day vividly. "Since the problem was caused by a trauma, and given her age, they both felt her problem is temporary. Time will heal her. She can speak. She talked a blue streak before Sara's death. But now the problem is, she's unwilling to speak. Without talking, therapy probably couldn't help her.''

Callie stared into the dying flames. "Something will bring her out. Sometimes people form habits they can't seem to break. They almost forget how it is to live without the behavior. Maybe Nattie's silence has become just that. Something has to happen to stimulate her, to make her want to speak and live like a normal child again.''

"I pray you're right.''

"Me, too.''

He rose and wandered to the fireplace. Peering at the embers, he lifted the poker and thrust at the red glow. Nattie needed to be prodded. She needed stimulus to wake her from her sadness. The flames stirred and sparks sprinkled from the burned wood. Could this spirited woman be the one to do that?

"You mentioned you'd like me to meet your daughter,'' Callie said.

He swung around to face her, realizing he had been lost in reverie. "Certainly,'' he said, embarrassed by his distraction.

"I'd like that, when you're ready.''

He glanced at the cup in her hand. "Are you finished with the tea?"

She took a final sip. "Yes, thanks. I have a two-hour drive home, and I'd like to get there before dark, if I can."

"I don't blame you. The winter roads can be treacherous."

He stood, and she rose and waited next to the chair, bathed in the warm glow of the fire. David studied her again. Her frame, though thin, rounded in an appealing manner and tugged at his memory. The straight skirt of her deep blue suit hit her modestly just below the knee. Covering a white blouse, the boxy jacket rested at the top of her hips. Her only jewelry was a gold lapel pin and earrings. She stepped to his side, and he calculated her height. Probably five foot five or six, he determined. He stood a head above her.

He stepped toward the doors, and she followed. In the foyer, he gestured to the staircase, and she moved ahead of him, gliding lightly up the steps, her skirt clinging momentarily to her shape as she took each step.

Awareness filled him. No wonder he'd wanted to hire an elderly woman. Ashamed of his own stirrings, he asked God for forgiveness. Instead of thinking of Nattie's needs, he'd struggled to protect his own vulnerability. He would learn to handle his emotions for his daughter's sake.

At the top of the stairs, he guided her down the hallway and paused outside a door. "Please don't expect much. She's not like the child God gave us."

His fingers grasped the knob, and Callie's soft, warm hand lowered and pressed against his.

"Please, don't worry," she said. "I understand hurt."

She raised her eyes to his, and a sense of fellowship like electricity charged through him, racing down to the extremity of his limbs. She lifted her hand, and he turned the knob.

He pushed the door open, and across the room, Nattie shifted her soft blue eyes toward them, then stared again at her knees.

Callie gaped, wide-eyed, at his child. Pulled into a tight knot, Nattie sat with her back braced against the bay enclosure, her feet resting on the window seat. The sun poured in through the pane and made flickering patterns on her pale skin. The same light filtered through her bright yellow hair.

Standing at Callie's side, David felt a shiver ripple through her body. He glimpsed at his child and then looked into the eyes of the virtual stranger, named Callie Randolph, whose face now flooded with compassion and love.

Chapter Four

Callie stared ahead of her at the frail vision on the window seat. She and David stood in Nattie's bedroom doorway for a moment, neither speaking. Finally he entered the room, approaching her like a father would a normal, happy child. "Nattie, this is Miss Randolph. She wants to meet you."

Callie moved as close to the silent child as she felt comfortable doing. "Hi, Nattie. I've heard nice things about you from your daddy. I brought you a present."

She detected a slight movement in the child's body at the word *present*. Hoping she'd piqued Nattie's interest, she opened her large shoulder bag and pulled out the books wrapped in colorful tissue and tied with a ribbon. "Here." She extended her hand holding the books.

Nattie didn't move, but sat with her arms bound to her knees.

Stepping forward, Callie placed the package by the

child's feet and backed away. She glanced at David. His gaze was riveted to his daughter.

He took a step forward and rested his hand on his daughter's shoulder. "Nattie, how about if you open the present?"

The child glanced at him, but made no move to respond.

David squeezed his large frame into the end of the window seat. He lifted the gift from the bench and raised it toward her.

She eyed the package momentarily, but then lowered her lids again, staring through the window as if they weren't there.

Frustration rose in Callie. The child's behavior startled her. A list of childhood illnesses raced through her mind. Then other thoughts took their place. How did Sara die? Was the child present at her death? Questions swirled in her thoughts. What might have happened in the past to trouble this silent child sitting rigidly on the window seat?

David relaxed and placed the package on his knees. "I'll open the gift for you, then, if you'd like." Tearing the paper from the gift, he lifted the books one by one, turning the colorful covers toward her. "'The Lost Lamb,'" he read, showing her the book.

Callie looked at the forlorn child and the book cover. If ever there were a lost lamb, it was Nattie. The next book he showed her was a child's New Testament in story form, and the last, children's poems. Nattie glanced at the book covers, a short-lived spark of interest on her face.

David placed the books again by her feet and rose,

his face tormented. Callie glanced at him and gestured to the window seat. "Do you mind?"

He shook his head, and she wandered slowly to the vacated spot and nestled comfortably in the corner. "I think I'd like to read this one," Callie said, selecting "The Lost Lamb," "if you don't mind." The child made no response. Callie searched David's face, but he seemed lost in thought.

Leaning back, Callie braced herself against the wall next to the window and opened the book. She glanced at Nattie, who eyed her without moving, and began to read. "'Oh my,' said Rebecca to her father, 'where is the new lamb?' Father looked into the pasture. The baby lamb was not in sight."

Callie directed the bright picture toward Nattie, who scanned the page, then returned her attention to her shoes. Callie continued. Nattie glimpsed at each picture without reaction. But, the child's minimal interest gave Callie hope. Patience, perseverance, attention, love—Callie would need all of those attributes if she were to work with this lost lamb.

Glancing from the book, she caught David easing quietly through the doorway. The story gained momentum, as Rebecca and her father searched the barnyard and the wooded hills for the stray. When they found the lamb, who had stumbled into a deep hole, Nattie's eyes finally stayed attentive to the page. When the lamb was again in Rebecca's arms, Callie heard a soft breath escape the child at her side. Nattie had, at least, listened to the story. A first success.

"That was a wonderful story, wasn't it? Sometimes when we feel so alone or afraid, we can remember that Jesus is always by our side to protect us, just like

Rebecca protected the lamb. I love stories like that one, don't you?" Callie rose. "Well, I have to go now, Nattie. But I hope to be back soon to read more stories with you."

She lay the book next to Nattie and gently caressed the child's jonquil-colored hair. Nattie's gaze lifted for a heartbeat, but this time when she lowered her eyes, she fastened her attention on the book.

Callie swallowed her building emotions and hurried from the room. She made her way down the stairs, and at the bottom, filled her lungs with refreshing air. When she released the healing breath, her body trembled.

"Thank you."

Callie's hand flew to her chest, she gasped and swung to her left. "Oh, you scared me."

David stood in the doorway across from the parlor where they had met. "You did a beautiful thing."

"She's a beautiful child, Mr. Hamilton. She breaks my heart, so I can only imagine how she breaks yours."

"Call me David, please. If we're going to live in the same house, 'Callie' and 'David' will sound less formal."

She faltered, her hand still knotted at her chest. *If we're going to live in the same house.* The meaning of his words registered, and she closed her eyes. He was asking her to stay. Could she? Would the experience break her heart once more? But suddenly, her own pain didn't matter. Her only thought was for the child sitting alone in an upstairs room.

Callie stepped toward him. "Yes, if we're going to live in the same house, I suppose you're right...

David. The 'David' will take some doing," she admitted with a faint grin.

He extended his hand. "I pray you'll make a difference in Nattie's life. In our lives, really. I see already you're a compassionate woman. I can ask for no more."

Callie accepted his hand in a firm clasp. "I hope you'll continue to feel like that." She eyed him, a knowing expression creeping on her face. "You've already seen me with my dander up, as they say." Her hand remained in his.

"Then we have nothing to worry about. I survived."

"Yes, you did. And quite admirably. Thank you for trusting in my...*youthful* abilities."

His hazel eyes captured hers and held her suspended until his words broke the spell. "It's my pleasure."

Callie gazed around her childhood bedroom, facing a new and frightening chapter in her life. Five times she had packed, heading for a patient's home. But tomorrow was different.

Nattie appeared in her mind, the child's face as empty of feeling as Callie's would be when she stepped into David Hamilton's home in Bedford. He was the last person she wanted to have know the fear that writhed inside her. She would step through the doorway with a charade of confidence. She had announced with no uncertainty that she could provide professional, compassionate care for Nattie. And she would.

The sound of Grace's unhappy voice echoed in

Callie's head. *"Bedford is too far away. Why must you be a live-in nurse? What if I need you? Dr. Swanson, right here in town, still needs an office nurse."* She'd heard the same questions and comments since she chose home-care. Tomorrow, another day—a new beginning.

Though she hadn't finished packing, Callie's thoughts dragged through her, sapping her energy. A good night's sleep would refresh her, she thought. With that notion, she crawled into bed.

But Callie couldn't escape her dream. It soon rose in her slumber, shrouded in darkness and mist.

In a foggy blur, his stare toyed with her, sweeping her body from head to toe, and her flush of excitement deepened to embarrassment. His smooth voice like a distant whisper echoed in her head. "Callie. That's a lovely, lovely name. Nearly pretty as you are, sweetheart."

An uneasy sensation rose in her, unexpected and unnatural. Why was he teasing her with his eyes? She felt self-conscious.

In the swirling darkness, he flashed his broad, charming smile, and his hushed voice touched her ear again. "You're nervous. No need to be nervous." He turned the bolt on the door.

The *click* of the lock cut through her sleep. Callie wrested herself from the blackness of her dream to the darkness of her room.

"Bedford's only a couple hours away, Mom. I told you already, I can get back here if you need me." Packing the last suitcase the next morning, Callie glanced over her shoulder at Grace. "I don't understand why you're worried. You've never needed me yet."

Grace leaned against the door frame. "Well, I get older every year. You never know." Grace's pinched expression gave witness to her unhappiness.

Callie bit back the words that could easily have sailed from her lips: *Only the good die young.* Her mother was well-meaning, she knew that, but Callie found a chip growing on her shoulder when she spent too much time with Grace. She needed to keep that situation in her prayers—only God could work a miracle.

Callie chuckled out loud. "We have the same problem, Mom. I seem to get older every year myself. Any idea how we can fix that?"

Grace's compressed features gave way to a grin. "Can't do much, I suppose. I just worry. Your sister lives thousands of miles away. Kenneth is useless. Sons don't care much about their mothers."

"If you need Ken, he can be here in a minute. But you have to call him and let him know. Men just aren't as attentive as women." Guilt swept over her. She hadn't been very attentive, either. And Grace was right—though she wasn't ready for the grave, they had celebrated her sixty-fifth birthday. And no one was getting any younger.

A sudden feeling of tenderness swept over her. She was her parents' "surprise" baby. At the age of forty, Grace had her "babies" raised. Patricia was fourteen, and Ken, eleven. Then came Callie, who was soon deemed the "little princess." All her parents' unfulfilled hopes and dreams were bundled into her. She had let them down with a bang.

A heavy silence hung in the room as Callie placed the last few items in her luggage. When she snapped the locks, she turned and faced her mother. "Well, I guess that's it. I may need a few other things, but I'm not that far away. And at this point, I'm not sure how long I'll be needed."

The words caught in her throat. Already, the face of Nattie loomed in her mind. Her greatest fear was beginning to take shape. This child would continue to linger in her thoughts when her job was completed in Bedford. And could she walk away from another child? She prayed she could handle it.

Grace stood at the doorway, her hands knotted in front of her. "You'll be coming back occasionally? So I'll see you once in a while, then?"

"Well, sure. I'm not chained to the house. At least, I don't think so." She grinned at Grace, trying to keep her parting light. Most of her previous patients had lived in the area. Living in Bedford would make trips home a bit more complicated.

Grace heaved a sigh and lifted her smaller bag. Callie grabbed the larger piece of luggage and followed her mother down the stairs and out the door.

As Callie loaded her car, she shuddered, thinking of her dream the night before. She drew the chilled, winter air through her lungs, clearing her thoughts. She stood for a moment, staring at the house where her parents had lived for most of her life, remembering...

When she returned inside, Grace had lunch waiting on the table. Seeing the food as another attempt to delay her, Callie wanted to say "no, thank you," but she had to eat somewhere. Noting her mother's forlorn expression, she sat at the table.

"Thanks, this will save time. I should arrive in Bedford in the mid-afternoon, if the weather cooperates. I'll have a chance to get settled before dinner." She bit into her sandwich.

Grace raised the tuna salad to her lips, then lowered it. "Are you sure you're safe with this man, Callie? He saw your references, but did you see his?"

Callie understood her mother's concern. "I think seeing his daughter is reference enough. He's not an outgoing, friendly man. I saw so much sadness in his eyes. Anyway, he has a full-time housekeeper who lives in. She looked comfortable enough. Though once I'm there, I imagine she'll enjoy having the opportunity to go home." Callie sipped her tea.

"You mean you have to keep house, too?"

Callie choked on her sip of tea. She quickly grabbed up her napkin to cover her mouth. "No, Mother. Agnes is from the community. She'll be able to go home and visit her family. Since I'm there, she won't have the responsibility to be the nanny. That's all. He says I'll have my own suite of rooms—bedroom, private bath and a little sitting room. And I'll have dinner with the family. Now, don't worry. I'll be fine."

Grace raised an eyebrow. "What kind of business is this man in to afford such a big home and all this help?"

"Limestone quarries and mills. They've been in the family for generations. His grandfather opened a quarry in the middle eighteen-hundreds, I think. Eventually his father took over."

"Family business, hmm? Must be a good one to keep generations at it."

"It is. I was really amazed. I picked up some brochures at the Chamber of Commerce office on my way out of town. So many famous buildings were made with Indiana limestone—the Pentagon, the Empire State Building, lots of buildings in Washington, D.C. So I'd say the family has enough money to get by."

Grace grinned. "To get by? I'd say. One of those aristocratic families...with money to throw away."

"Not really. It's a beautiful house, but David seems down to earth."

"David? What's this 'David' business?"

"Mother." Callie rolled her eyes, yet heat rose up her neck at her mother's scrutiny. "Since we're living in the same house, I suppose he thought 'Miss Randolph' and 'Mr. Hamilton' sounded too formal."

"A little formality never hurt anybody."

"I'm an employee, Mom. And he has no interest in me. The man's not over the death of his wife."

"Accident?"

Callie's brows knitted. "I don't know. He didn't say, and I didn't ask. I'd already asked too many questions for someone who was supposed to be the person interviewed."

"Never hurts to ask questions."

"I'm sure I'll find out one of these days. And I don't expect to be with him much. Mainly dinner. He'll be gone some of the time, traveling for his business. I'm there to be with Natalie. Nattie, they call her. She's a beautiful child."

"Just keep your eyes focused on the child, hear me?"

Callie shook her head. "Yes, Mother. I think I've learned to take care of myself."

She caught a flicker of reminiscence in Grace's expression, and froze, praying she wouldn't stir up the past. Grace bit her tongue, and Callie changed the subject.

"The area is lovely there, all covered with snow. And imagine spring. The trees and wildflowers. And autumn. The colored leaves—elms, maples, birches."

An uneasy feeling rippled down her back. Would she see the autumn colors? Nattie needed to be ready for school. If the child was back to normal by then, her job would be finished.

"It's snowing," Grace said, pulling Callie from her thoughts. "And hard."

"Then, I'd better get moving." Callie gulped down her last bite and drained the teacup.

Without fanfare, she slipped on her coat and said goodbye. She needed to be on her way before she was snowbound. Time was fleeting, and so was her sanity.

Chapter Five

David sat with his face in his hands, his elbows resting on his large cherry wood desk. The day pressed in from all sides. Callie should arrive any time now. He'd expected her earlier, yet the uncooperative weather had apparently slowed her travel.

The day of her interview lingered in his memory. Though Nattie had responded minimally to Callie's ministrations, David was grateful for the most insignificant flicker of interest from his daughter these days. Callie had brought about that infinitesimal moment.

The major concern that lodged in his gut was himself. He feared Callie. She stirred in him remembrances he didn't want to face and emotions he had avoided for two years. His only solution was to avoid her—keep his distance.

Though often quiet, Sara had had her moments of liveliness and laughter. He recalled their spring walks on the hill and a warm, sunny day filled with play when she dubbed him "Sir Knight" with a daisy chain she'd made. Wonderful moments rose in his mind of Sara playing pat-a-cake with Nattie or singing children's songs.

If he let Callie's smiles and exuberance get under his skin, he might find himself emotionally tangled. Until Nattie was well, and he dealt with his personal sorrow, he had no interest in any kind of relationship—and he would live with that decision. But he wished wisdom had been his gatekeeper when he'd extended her the job with such enthusiasm.

On top of it all, today they would celebrate Nattie's sixth birthday. Tension caught between his shoulder blades when he pictured the occasion: a cake with candles she wouldn't blow out, gifts she wouldn't open, and joy she wouldn't feel.

David was reminded of the day Sara had surprised him for his birthday with tickets to see Shakespeare's darkest, direst play, *King Lear*. Yet, he'd accompanied her, looking pleased and interested so as not to hurt the woman he loved so deeply.

But Nattie would not look interested to please him. She wouldn't say "thank you" or force a smile. The lack of response for the gift was not what hurt. She appeared to feel nothing, and that tore at his very fiber.

His wife's death had been no surprise; Nattie's living death was.

Rising from his chair, David wandered to the window and pulled back the draperies. The snow piled against the hedges and mounded against the edge of the driveway. Lovely, pure white at this moment, the snow would soon become drab and monotonous like his life.

A flash of headlights caught the mounds of crystal flakes and glowed with diamond-like sparkles. David's heart surged, and for a heartbeat, he held his breath. Dropping the edge of the drapery, he spun toward the doorway. She would need help bringing in her luggage. He could, at least, do that.

Callie climbed the snow-covered stairs with care and rang the bell. When the door opened, her stomach somersaulted. Her focus fell upon David Hamilton, rather than Agnes. "Oh," she said, knowing her face registered surprise, "I expected Agnes." Her amazement was not so much at seeing him at the door as feeling her stomach's unexpected acrobatics.

"I was keeping an eye out for you, concerned about the weather." His face appeared drawn and serious.

"Thank you. The drive was a bit tense."

He stepped back and held the door open for her.

She glanced at his darkened face. "I hope nothing is wrong. You look…" Immediately she was sorry she had spoken. Perhaps his stressed appearance had to do with *her*—hiring someone "so young," as he had continually reminded her.

"I'm fine," he said, looking past her toward the automobile. "Let me get my jacket, and we can bring in your luggage."

He darted to the entrance closet, and in a brief moment, joined her.

Heading down the slippery porch stairs, Callie's eyes filled with his Titan stature. In her preoccupation, her foot missed the center of the step and skidded out from under her. She crumpled backward, reaching out to break her fall.

David flung his hand behind her and caught her in the crook of his arm, while the other hand swung around to hold her secure. "Careful," he cautioned.

Captured in his arms, his gaze locked with hers, she wavered at the sensation that charged through her. She marveled at his vibrant hazel eyes in the dusky light.

"Be careful. You could get hurt," he repeated, setting her on her feet.

She found her voice and mumbled a "thank you."

Capturing her elbow, he helped her down the next two steps. When she opened the trunk, he scanned its contents.

"I'll help you in with the luggage," he said, "and I'll come back for the rest."

She nodded. Hearing his commanding voice, she couldn't disagree. He handed her the smallest case, taking the larger himself, and they climbed the steps with care.

Once inside, David set down the larger case and addressed Agnes, who was waiting in the foyer. "Show Callie her rooms, please. I'll carry in the boxes and bring them up."

Agnes nodded and grabbed the larger case. But when David stepped outside, Callie took the case from her. "Please, let me carry this one. It's terribly heavy."

Agnes didn't argue and grasped the smaller case, then headed up the stairs. At the top, the housekeeper walked down the hallway and stopped at a door to the left, across from Nattie's room. She turned the knob and stepped aside.

As Callie entered, her heart skipped a beat. She stood in the tower she had admired from outside. The sitting room was fitted with a floral chintz love seat and matching chair of vibrant pinks and soft greens, with a lamp table separating the grouping. A small oak desk sat along one curved wall, and oak bookshelves rose nearby. A woman's touch was evident in the lovely decor.

Callie dropped her luggage and darted to the center window, pulling back the sheer white curtains framed by moss-colored draperies. She gazed outside at the scene. A light snow floated past the window, and below, David pulled the last carton from the trunk and closed the lid. He hefted the box into the air, then disappeared beneath the porch roof.

Agnes remained by the door, and when Callie turned back and faced the room, the housekeeper gestured through the doorway to the bedroom. Callie lifted her luggage and followed her inside. The modest bedroom, too, illustrated a feminine hand. Delicate pastel flowers sprinkled the wallpaper that ended at the chair-molding. Below, the color of palest blue met a deeper blue carpet.

"Agnes, this is beautiful." She wanted to ply the woman with questions about Sara and how she used the charming rooms.

"Mr. Hamilton hoped you'd like it."

"How could I not? It's lovely. So dainty and feminine."

Agnes nodded and directed her to a door that opened to a walk-in closet; across the room, another door led to a pristine private bathroom, graced by a claw-foot bathtub.

As she spun around to take in the room once again, David came through the doorway with the box.

''Bricks?'' he asked.

''Nearly. Books and things.''

''Ah, I should have guessed. Then you'd like this in the sitting room.''

''Please.'' Callie followed him through the doorway.

David placed the box between the desk and the bookshelves. ''I'll be right back with the other. Much lighter, I'm happy to say.''

Callie grinned. ''No books.''

He left the room, and she returned to Agnes, who hovered in the doorway.

''Miss Randolph, did you want me to help unpack your things?''

''Oh, no, Agnes, I can get it. And please call me Callie. The 'Miss' stuff makes me nervous.'' She gave the woman a pleasant look, but received only a nod in return.

''Then I'll get back to the kitchen,'' Agnes said as she edged her way to the door.

''Yes, thank you.''

Agnes missed David by a hairbreadth as he came through the doorway with the last box. He held it and glanced at Callie.

''Bedroom,'' Callie said, before he asked, and she gestured to the adjoining room.

David turned with his burden and vanished through the doorway. Before she could follow, he returned.

"So, I hope you'll be comfortable here. I still want to get a television for you. But you do have a radio."

Callie's focus followed the direction of his hand. A small clock radio sat on the desk. "The rooms are lovely. Just beautiful. Did your wif—Sara decorate them? They have a woman's touch."

"Yes," he said, nodding his head at the sitting room. "She used this as her reading room, and she slept here if she worried about Nattie's health. The bedroom was the baby's nursery then."

"I couldn't ask for a nicer place to stay. Thank you."

He glanced around him, edging backward toward the door, his hands moving nervously at his sides. "Then I'll let you get unpacked and settled. Dinner will be at six. We're celebrating this evening. We have a couple of guests for Nattie's birthday."

"Really? I'm glad I'm here for the celebration. And pleased I brought along a couple of small presents. I'd be embarrassed to attend her birthday party empty-handed." She kept her voice level and free of the irritation that prickled her. Why hadn't he thought to tell her about the birthday?

"I'm sorry. I should have mentioned it." A frown flashed over his face, yet faded as if another thought crossed his mind. He stepped toward the door. "I'll see you at dinner."

He vanished through the doorway before Callie could respond. She stared into the empty space, wondering what had driven him so quickly from the room.

Glancing at her wristwatch, the time read four-thirty. She had an hour-and-a-half before dinner. She needed time to dress appropriately if they were celebrating Nattie's birthday.

The word *birthday* took her back. Nattie was six today, so close in age to her own child, who had turned six on Christmas Day. Her chest tightened as the fingers of memory squeezed her heart. Could she protect herself from loving this child too deeply? And why did Natalie have to be six? Eight, four…any other age might not have bothered her as much.

She dropped on the edge of the bed and stared at the carpet. With an inner ache, she asked God to give her compassion and patience. Compassion for Nattie, and patience with herself.

As he waited for Callie's entrance, David prepared his guests for her introduction. Reverend John Spier listened attentively, and his sister Mary Beth bobbed her head, as if eager to meet someone new in the small town of Bedford.

"How nice," Mary Beth said, lowering her eyelids shyly at David. "Since I've come to help John in the parsonage, I've not met too many young unmarried women. Most people my age have already settled down. I look forward to our meeting."

"Yes, I hoped Callie might enjoy meeting you, too."

"Although once John finds a proper bride, I assume I'll go back to Cleveland…unless God has other plans."

David cringed inwardly, noticing the young woman's hopeful look, and wondered if he'd made a mistake inviting the pastor and his younger sister to the birthday dinner. The evening could prove to be difficult enough, depending on Nattie's disposition.

Looking toward the doorway, David saw Callie descending the staircase. "Here's Callie, now. Excuse me." David made for the doorway.

By the time Callie had reached the first floor, he was at the foot of the staircase. Caught off guard by her attractiveness, David gazed at her burgundy wool dress adorned with a simple string of pearls at her neck. The deep red of her gown emphasized the flush in her cheeks and highlighted the golden tinges of her honey-colored hair. As he focused his gaze, their eyes met, and her blush heightened.

"I see the party has already begun," she said. "I heard your voices as I came down the stairs."

"Now that you've joined us, everyone's here but the guest of honor." A sigh escaped him before he could harness it. "I invited our new pastor and his sister. I thought you might like to meet some of the younger people in town." He motioned for her to precede him. "We're in the living room."

She stepped around him, and he followed, watching the fullness of the skirt swish around her legs as she walked. The movement entranced him. Passing through the doorway at her side, he pulled his attention from her shapely legs to his guests.

As she entered the room, John's face brightened, and he rose, meeting her with his outstretched hand. "You're Callie."

"Yes, and you're David's pastor."

"John Spier," he said, then turned with a flourish. "And this is my sister, Mary Beth Spier."

"It's nice to meet you," Callie said, glancing at them both.

The young woman shot Callie an effusive grin. "And I'm certainly pleased to meet you. Being new in town myself, I've been eager to meet some young woman who—"

"Have a seat, Callie." David gestured to the love seat. Interrupting Mary Beth was rude, but he couldn't bear to hear her announce again that she was one of the few single women in town. David chided himself. He should have used more sense than to invite a young woman to dinner who apparently saw him as a possible husband.

When he joined Callie on the love seat, she shifted closer to the arm and gracefully crossed her legs. His attention shifted to her slim ankles, then to her fashionable gray-and-burgundy brushed-leather pumps.

John leaned back in his chair and beamed. "I hope we'll see you at church on Sundays. We're a small congregation, but loaded with spirit. Although we could use a benefactor to help us with some much-needed repairs." His glance shot toward David.

David struggled with the grimace that crept to his face, resulting, he was sure, in a pained smile. "Agnes will announce dinner shortly. Then I'll go up and see if I can convince Nattie to join us. I never know how she'll respond." He eyed them, wondering if they understood. "I've had a difficult time here since Sara... Well, let's not get into that."

He wished he would learn to tuck his sorrow somewhere other than his shirtsleeve. He turned his attention to Callie. "Would you care for some mulled cider?"

She agreed, and he poured a mug of the warm brew. He regarded her full, rosy lips as she took a sip. She pulled away from the rim and nodded her approval.

His mind raced, inventing conversation. Tonight he felt tired, and wished he could retire to his study and spend the evening alone.

When Pastor John spoke, David felt himself relax.

"So where do you hail from, Callie?"

Without hesitation, she related a short personal history. Soon, Mary Beth joined in. David listened, pressing himself against the cushions rather than participating.

To his relief, Agnes announced dinner.

"Well, finally," David said, embarrassed at his obvious relief. David climbed the stairs to find Nattie, as Callie and the guests proceeded toward the dining room.

Callie held back and followed David's ascent with her eyes. He was clearly uncomfortable. She wondered if it was his concern for Nattie or the obvious flirtations of Mary Beth.

In the dining room, Agnes indicated David's seating arrangement. Mary Beth's focus darted from Callie to Agnes; she was apparently wondering if the housekeeper had made an error. She was not seated next to David.

When he arrived back with Nattie clinging to his side, he surveyed the table without comment. Except for a glance at Callie, the child kept her eyes downcast. David pulled out her chair, and Nattie slid onto it, focusing on the folded napkin on her plate, her hands below the table. David sat and asked Pastor John to offer the blessing.

Callie lowered her eyes, but in her peripheral vision she studied Nattie's reaction to the scene around her. Until David said "Amen," Nattie's eyes remained closed, but when she raised her lids, she glimpsed around the table almost without moving her head.

When her focus settled on Callie, their gazes locked.

In that moment, something special happened. Would she call the fleeting glimmer—hope, premonition or fact? Callie wasn't sure. But a sweet tingle rose from the base of her spine to the tips of her fingers. Never before had she felt such a sensation.

Chapter Six

After dinner, Nattie withdrew, staring into space and mentally recoiling from those who addressed her. David blew the lit candles on her cake as they sang "Happy Birthday" and excused her before the gifts were opened, saying she needed to rest. The wrapped packages stood ignored like eager young ladies dressed in their finery for the cotillion, but never asked to dance.

Callie longed to go with the child to the second floor, but refrained from suggesting it. Tonight was her first evening in the house, so she was still a stranger. And Nattie needed her father.

After they left the room, Callie sat uneasily with the Spiers, lost in her own thoughts.

"Such a shame about the little girl," John said, looking toward the doorway. "Has she always been so withdrawn?"

With effort, Callie returned to the conversation.

"Since her mother died a couple of years ago. I'm sure she'll be herself in time."

Mary Beth sighed and murmured. "Such a shame. And poor David having to carry the burden all alone."

John turned sharply to his sister, his words a reprimand. "Mary Beth, we're never alone. God is always with us."

"Oh, John, I know the Lord is with us. I meant, he has no wife." Her look pleaded for forgiveness, and she lowered her eyes.

Callie didn't miss Mary Beth's less-than-subtle meaning. "I don't think you need to worry about David. He'll come through this a stronger person, I'm sure. And don't forget, Mary Beth..."

The young woman looked curiously at Callie. "Don't forget...?"

"David's not alone anymore. I'm here to help him."

Mary Beth paled, and a flush rose to Callie's cheeks. Callie raised her hand nonchalantly to her face, feeling the heat. Her comment astounded her. She sounded like a woman fighting for her man.

When David returned to the parlor, the guests rose to leave, and Callie took advantage of their departure to say good-night and head for her room. Confusion drove her up the stairs. She felt protective and possessive of this family—not only of Nattie, but of David. In less than a day, the situation already tangled in her heart.

Callie woke with the morning light dancing on the flowered wallpaper. She looked around the room, confused for a moment, and wondered where she was. Then she remembered. She slid her legs over the edge of the bed and sat, collecting her thoughts. How should she begin? What could she do to help this child, now bound in a cocoon, to blossom like a lovely butterfly?

One thing she knew. The process would take time. She stepped down to the soft, lush carpet and padded to the bathroom. A shower would awaken her body and her mind, she hoped.

When she finished dressing, she steadied herself, knowing what she had to do wouldn't be easy. She bowed her head, asking for God's wisdom and guidance, then left her room to face her first day.

Across the hall, Nattie's door stood open. Callie glimpsed inside. The child again sat on the window seat, but this time was looking at one of the books Callie had given her. Suddenly, she lifted her head and connected with Callie's gaze.

With her eyes focused on Nattie, Callie breathed deeply and strode purposefully to the doorway. "Well, good morning. Look at the wonderful sunshine."

Nattie followed her movement, but her face registered no response.

"When I woke, I saw the sun dance on my walls. I bet you did, too."

Nattie's attention darted to her wallpaper and back again to Callie. Was it tension or curiosity Callie saw settling there? She longed for a cup of coffee, but she'd made her move, and she'd stick it out. When she ambled toward the window seat, Nattie recoiled slightly. Callie only leaned over and glanced out the window. Nattie calmed.

"Did you look outside? The sun has turned the snow into a world of sparkling diamonds. And I've been told 'diamonds are a girl's best friend.'" She giggled lightheartedly, hoping Nattie would relax. "That's pretty silly, isn't it. I think the *snow* is a girl's best friend. Maybe we could take a walk outside today. We might even make a snowman."

Callie saw Nattie turn toward the window and scan the fresh, glistening snow. She had piqued the child's interest.

"Nattie, I imagine you had breakfast already." She looked for some kind of response. None. "I'll go down and have a bite to eat. If you'd like to go outside, you can put on some warm stockings before I return. How's that?" Callie swung through the doorway with a wave and headed toward the stairs.

Would the child have the stockings on when she returned? If Nattie didn't want to talk, Callie would find another way to communicate until the child trusted her. Callie's thoughts thundered with questions. But mainly, she wanted to learn about Sara's death.

Silence filled the lower level of the house. She followed the aroma of breakfast and entered the dining room, where a lone table setting waited for her. She filled a plate with scrambled eggs and bacon from a small chafing dish, and poured a cup of coffee. This morning she didn't feel like eating alone. Looking for company, she carried the plate and cup through the door leading to the kitchen.

She found herself inside a butler's pantry, but

through an arch, she spotted a stove and counter. Sounds emanated from that direction, and she headed through the doorway.

Agnes spun around, flinging her hand to her heart.

"Sorry, Agnes. I scared you."

The housekeeper's wide eyes returned to normal. "I didn't expect anyone, that's all. Can I get you something? I left your breakfast in the—" Her gaze lowered. "Oh, I see you have your plate."

Callie placed her dish and cup on the broad oak table. "Do you mind if I eat in here with you, Agnes? I don't feel like eating alone this morning."

Agnes appeared flustered. She rushed forward with a damp cloth to wipe the already spotless table.

"I'm not trying to make work for you. The table's fine. I just thought you and I could get to know each other a little better. We're both employees here, and I'm sure familiarity can make our days more pleasant."

Agnes eyed her for a moment, then her face relaxed. "I sort of keep my place around here. Behind the scenes. You're more involved with Mr. Hamilton and Natalie. Except recently, while Mr. Hamilton looked for someone. But I'm at a loss. I never quite knew what to do for the child." She took a deep breath.

"Do you have a moment to join me in a cup of coffee?" Callie motioned to the empty chair across from her.

Agnes glanced at the chair, then at Callie. "Why, I don't mind if I do." She poured herself a mug of coffee from the warming pot and slipped onto the chair. "Black," she said, raising the mug. "I drink it black."

"Never could drink coffee black, myself. I like a little milk. I say 'cream,' but I prefer milk really." Callie smiled, and for the first time received a sincere smile in return. "So you've been here only a half year, if I remember correctly."

"Yes, about seven months now."

"I suppose following in Miriam's shadow was difficult."

Agnes nodded vigorously. "Oh yes, very hard. Miriam was part of this family forever. She's a wonderful woman. I knew her from church—Mr. Hamilton's church. That's how he knew me. When Miriam had to retire, he asked if I might be interested in the job. I'd been working for a family that had recently moved. Sort of destined, I suppose."

"Do you like working here?" In Callie's view, Agnes seemed to tiptoe around the house. The image didn't imply comfortable working conditions.

"Mr. Hamilton pays me well, and I'm always treated with respect."

Callie eyed her. "But you don't like working here."

Agnes fidgeted for a moment. "It's not that I don't like it here. The place isn't really homey, if you know what I mean. Mr. Hamilton has his moods. He's quiet and so is the child. Like the house is filled with shadows. He travels a lot, and I struggle to relate to the poor little thing upstairs. Yet whether he's here or not, she doesn't seem to notice one way or the other." She paused, drawing in a deep breath. "Now I don't mean Mr. Hamilton doesn't love his child. I'm sure he does.''

''Don't apologize, Agnes. I know what you mean. Sometimes he seems as withdrawn as Nattie. Once in a while, I sense a chink in his wall, but he mends it as quickly as it appears.''

Agnes's head bobbed again. ''You do understand.''

Callie nibbled on a piece of bacon. She was filled with curiosity. ''Did you know Mrs. Hamilton?''

''So lovely. Yes, she played the church organ.''

''The church organ? Well, that explains some things.'' Callie recalled David's comment about music.

''Such a sad thing, when she died.''

Callie's pulse skipped through her veins. ''You know how she died, then? I wasn't told.''

''She was sick for a time. Cancer. They weren't married very long...maybe six or seven years. Such a shame.''

Callie shook her head at the thought of someone dying so young. ''I wonder what caused Nattie to withdraw so badly. All children are close to their mothers, but her behavior seems so unusual. Odd, really.''

''Wondered that myself. I didn't know the family real well. Just Sundays, that's all, and being a small town, you hear about troubles. They were a happy family until the missus got sick.''

''I'll ask Mr. Hamilton sometime, but I don't want to sound nosy. If I had a clue to Nattie's problem, I'd have someplace to begin with her.''

Callie rose and placed her empty plate and cup in the sink. ''Mr. Hamilton is at work, I suppose.''

"Yes, he left early this morning. Probably relieved you were here."

"I'm hoping to coax Nattie outside. She's in her room too much. She needs fresh air."

"That'd be nice. I hope she goes out with you."

"Me, too," Callie said, wondering what to do if her plan didn't work.

When she returned to the second floor, she found Nattie on the floor with a puzzle. Her feet were tucked beneath her, so Callie couldn't see her stockings. She scanned the room and saw a pair lying discarded on the floor. Her stomach flip-flopped. Had the child put on the thick ones?

"I'm back," Callie called as she made her entrance.

Nattie glanced at her, then turned her attention to the odd-shaped puzzle pieces spread out on the floor. Callie wandered in and sat next to her on the carpet. The child withdrew her hand for a moment, glancing at Callie with a slight frown, then changed her mind and continued to locate the pieces.

Callie didn't speak, but searched until she found a piece, then placed it in the correct spot. They continued until the last piece remained. Callie waited, letting Nattie fit in the last of the puzzle.

"That's wonderful, Nattie, and you got to put in the last piece. I love to find the last piece." She tittered, hoping to gain some reaction from the child.

Instead, Nattie slid the puzzle aside and pulled her feet out in front of her.

Relief spilled over Callie. The child had donned thicker stockings. "Good. I see you want to go outside. Now, it's my turn to get ready. Would you like to come with me to my room?'' Callie rose, but Nattie remained where she was. ''Okay, then, you wait here, and I'll be back in a minute. You'll need a sweater, too, to wear under your coat.''

She slipped quickly from the room to collect her warm coat and gloves, and hoped she could find Nattie's coat, boots and gloves somewhere. She'd ask Agnes.

David pulled down the driveway as dusk settled. Once again, he'd put in a long workday. The sky had faded to a grayish purple, and the ripples of glistening snow he had admired early in the morning now looked dull and shadowed. As he neared the house, he felt a twinge at his nerve endings, and he applied the brake and peered at the snow-covered lawn.

Sets of footprints had trampled through the snow. He shifted into park and opened his door, intrigued by the sight of the boot marks. The woman's print would have meant little, but beside the larger indentions, he saw the smaller footprint of his daughter.

In a trance-like state, he followed the prints that wove through the evergreens and around the elms. In an open area, he paused. On the ground, he stared at imprints of angels. Heads, wings and bodies pressed into the snow. But, sadly, all adult angels. No seraphim or cherubim. No Nattie. Only the impression of the household's newest employee stamped a design into the fresh snow.

Yet a bright thought pierced his disappointment. Though Nattie had not made an angel, she had been outside and had walked in the snow—more progress in one day than he had seen in months. He should be grateful for each small gift.

He looked again at the fanned angel impressions at his feet. He counted three, four. He pictured the young woman, flinging herself to the ground, flailing her arms and legs to amuse his silent child. Callie's laughter rang in his mind. Angel? Yes, perhaps God had sent a human angel to watch over his daughter.

He dashed to the car and drove the short distance to the house. His eager feet carried him up the steps, and when he opened the front door, the house had come alive. In place of the usual silence, music played softly from a radio or television program in the parlor, and with anticipation he glanced into the room before hanging his coat. Callie sat curled on the sofa with her feet tucked beneath her, a book in her hand.

She heard him, for she raised her eye from the book, and a playful look covered her face. "Hello. You're home late this evening."

From the doorway, he stared at her in the firelight, his coat still clutched in his hand. "Too often, I'm afraid."

"Let me take your coat, Mr. Hamilton."

David jumped slightly and turned apologetically to Agnes. "Oh, thanks." After he released his coat to her care, he strode into the parlor, his eyes riveted to the firelight glinting on Callie's golden-brown hair.

He fell into the chair across from her. "I noticed a slight miracle outside when I came up the driveway."

Her lips parted in an easy smile. "The angels?"

Watching the animation on her face, he nodded.

"Only mine, I'm afraid. I tried." She lifted a bookmark, slid it between the pages and closed the volume.

"Oh, don't feel discouraged. Nattie went outside with you. We haven't been able to move her beyond these doors. In one day, you've worked wonders. I'm amazed."

Her eyes brightened. "I'm pleased then. I thought I was a minimal failure."

"Not at all." A scent of beef and onions drifted through the doorway and his stomach growled. "You've eaten?"

"No." She shook her head, and her hair glistened in the light. "I waited for you."

"That's nice."

"But Nattie ate, I'm afraid."

"Let me run up and see her, and I'll hurry right down." He rose and dashed up the stairway.

Callie watched him hurry away and filled with sadness, thinking of his excitement over something as simple as his child's walk in the snow. Her attention fell to her lap and the book that lay there.

Then his words rang in her head, and she raised her hand to her chest to calm the fluttering from within. "That's nice," he'd said, when she told him she'd waited for supper. Callie closed her eyes. Why did she care what he said? She was an employee doing her job. That was all.

His footsteps left the oriental carpet and hit the shiny wood floor at the entrance to the parlor, and she looked toward the doorway.

"Agnes says dinner is ready," he said.

She rose, and as they neared the dining room, the aroma stirred her hunger. A low rumble from her stomach echoed in the hallway. She glanced at him apologetically.

"Don't feel bad. My stomach isn't complaining loudly, but I'm starving. You shouldn't have waited, but I'm glad you did."

A flush of excitement rose in her, until she heard his next sentence.

"I'm anxious to hear about your day with Nattie."

I'm being foolish. Lord, keep my mind focused on my purpose in this home. Not on silly thoughts. Her flush deepened in her embarrassment, and she hoped he might not notice in the softened light of the dining room doorway.

As they stepped into the room, Agnes came through the kitchen entrance with a steaming platter. She placed it on the table, then hit the switch as she exited, brightening the lights above the table.

David pulled out a chair for Callie, and she sat, waiting for him to be seated. The platter, sitting before them, aroused her senses. A mound of dark roasted beef was surrounded by sauteed onions, browned potatoes and carrots. She bowed her head to murmur a silent prayer, but before she asked God's blessing, David's warm voice split the silence.

He offered thanks for the food and the day, then he thanked God for Callie's presence in the house. A heated blush rose again to her cheeks. Now in the brightened room, when David looked up from his prayer, she knew her pink cheeks glowed.

"Sorry," Callie said, touching her cheeks, "I'm not used to being blessed along with a roast."

An unexpected burst of laughter rolled from David's chest. Agnes halted in the doorway, balancing a gravy boat and a salad bowl in apparent surprise. She looked from David to Callie, then added a smile to her face as she approached the table.

"This roast looks and smells wonderful, Agnes," David said, the merriment still lingering in his tone.

"Why, thank you, Mr. Hamilton." She placed the items on the table and scurried from the room with a final wide-eyed glance over her shoulder.

"Poor Agnes hasn't heard much laughter in the house since she came. I think I've surprised her." His hazel eyes crinkled at the edges as he looked at Callie.

"Then it's about time," Callie said lightly, trying to ignore the beating pulse in her temples. "'Laughter is good for all that ails you,' my father used to say."

"He was right. Laughter is music everyone can sing."

The word *music* seemed to catch them both off guard, and they each bent over their plates, concentrating on filling their stomachs. They ate quietly, keeping their eyes directed at the meat and potatoes. Callie searched her mind for something to draw him out again and distract her own thoughts.

"I borrowed a book from the library. What a lovely room. And so many wonderful books." She pictured the room next to the library. She'd turned the knob, but the door had been locked. Though curious what the room was, she didn't ask. "I hope you don't mind about the book."

"No, not at all. You're welcome to read every one."

"I'd have to live here forever to do that."

He lifted his eyes to hers. "Yes, I suppose you would."

Silence lingered again, until David asked about Nattie. The rest of the meal was filled with tales of Callie's day with the child. They both were comfortable with the topic, and the conversation flowed easily until the meal ended.

When they reentered the foyer, she said good-night and climbed the stairs. But the *click* of a door lock startled her, and she spun around. David slipped quietly into the room at the bottom of the stairs. Another faint *click* told her he had locked himself in. The sound bolted her to the floor, as her dreams rose up to haunt her. She stood a moment until she gained composure, then continued up the stairs.

Chapter Seven

After breakfast, Callie knocked on Nattie's door. Since the day in the snow, two weeks had passed with no new breakthrough.

Today, Nattie sat staring out the window with a doll in her lap. Pieces of doll clothing lay at her side, and Callie sensed she had stopped in mid-play. The doll wore a diaper and dress, with the shoes and bonnet waiting in a pile.

Nattie glanced at Callie, but turned her attention to the doll. Callie ambled to the window seat and sat for a moment before she spoke. "What a pretty baby you have there. But the poor child is only half dressed. What about her shoes and bonnet?"

Nattie ignored Callie, though occasionally she looked curiously at her and then lowered her eyes again.

Callie wondered what would make a difference. How could she get through to the lonely little girl. "Would you like to color? Or maybe we could draw some pictures?'' Nothing. Whatever she encouraged Nattie to do, Callie would first do it alone. That much she had learned. She shifted to the floor and pulled out one of Nattie's puzzles. Tumbling the pieces onto the floor, she turned them so all the picture pieces were facing up.

Nattie glanced at her, swiveling so her legs dangled over the window seat. She lay the doll to the side and watched.

Callie began forming the outer rim of the puzzle. When the frame was nearly complete, Nattie slid from the bench and joined her. She peered at the pieces to see if the fit matched, and often they did. Each time the child joined her, Callie felt they had made some progress.

Callie hummed a tune as she worked the puzzle. The sound surprised her. Humming, like singing, had vanished from her life. Today she felt like murmuring the simple melody, and best of all, Nattie eyed her more than usual. The child seemed comforted by the droning sound. Certainly her mother had hummed to her, too. Perhaps the memory soothed her.

Eventually, Callie rose and stared outside. The past days had seemed lonely. David had gone to Atlanta on a business trip, and except for an occasional conversation with Agnes, her world was as silent as Nattie's.

March would be along shortly, and she longed for warmer weather when she and Nattie could go for walks and run in the fresh air. Maybe then the child would warm the same way the summer sun would heat the soil, encouraging new shoots to sprout. Nattie, too, might come alive again.

* * *

As David finished his breakfast, Callie entered the dining room. Each time she appeared, a deep longing filled him.

"Good morning," she said brightly, and turned to the buffet.

David returned her greeting and watched as she took a plate and scooped up a serving spoonful of scrambled eggs. With toast and sausage on her plate, she sat on David's left. "How was your trip?"

"Fine. Too long actually, but that's business."

They hadn't talked much recently. All he'd learned was that nothing dramatic had occurred as yet with regard to Nattie. Though his hopes remained high, the process seemed to be taking forever.

"I wouldn't know much about business. I've always been a nurse. Whole different career. Though, we notice how quiet it is when you're away." She lowered her eyes, focusing on her plate and scooping egg onto her fork.

David knew exactly what she meant. Before she had come, the house had seemed a tomb. He sipped his coffee, hating to tell her he would be gone again that evening.

"I have a dinner invitation this evening, so I won't be home. I suppose you can endure one more night without my tantalizing conversation."

As he spoke, her face faded to disappointment. "One more night, huh? When I took the job I didn't have any guarantees of dinner entertainment, so I suppose I can handle it." She put a smile on her face, but David had learned enough about Callie to know the smile was to appease him.

He folded his napkin and laid it next to his plate. "To be honest, I'd rather stay home."

"Business dinner?"

"Probably, but on the pretense of a social evening at the parsonage."

Callie's face gave way to a wry grin. "Ah, an invitation from Mary Beth, no doubt."

A sigh escaped him before he could control it. "No doubt." He eyed his wristwatch and rose, longing to stay and talk. He had forgotten how comfortable it was to sit after a meal and chat. He and Sara had often lingered at the table long after the meal was finished. He could easily do the same with Callie. But his business waited him. "I'd better be on my way."

"I'm sure you'll have fun." Callie tilted her face toward him, and her words sounded to David as if they wavered between sarcasm and wit.

"How about a wager?"

"Sorry, kind sir, I don't make bets. It's sinful, you know."

Her smile sent a tingle through him, and he glanced at his face as he passed a mirror in the entry to see if the unexpected sensation showed.

"I suppose we should have been polite and invited Callie to join us," Mary Beth gushed, after they settled into the cozy living room after dinner. "I don't know where my mind was."

I do, David thought as he gallantly tried to smile at her comment. "I'm sure she understands." Thinking of Callie's wry smile, he realized she understood Mary Beth Spier was looking for a husband—but in the wrong direction.

"Perhaps next time," John said. "We should enjoy each other's company more often. Other than Sundays, I might add."

David enjoyed his private joke. If John were to be perfectly honest, he might also add that he didn't see David on many Sundays, either. David waited, wondering where John was going from there.

"Speaking of Sundays," John said, "we certainly miss having an organ for worship. Looking back at the records, I see your wife was the organist for a couple of years."

David gathered his wits, keeping his face unemotional. "Yes, she was. I believe a lady named Ruta Dryer filled in for my wife while she was ill...and after Sara died."

"Yes, I noticed that, too. But then the organ needed some work, and I'm afraid financially we haven't been able to make those repairs."

"I see," David said, waiting for the pitch.

"I wonder if you'd considered helping out with that little project. I imagine we could find an organist—but first, we need the instrument."

David bit his lip, struggling to control his emotions. "Sara's death was a tremendous loss for my daughter and me, as you can imagine. I haven't given much thought to the organ since then. I've been concerned about my child, and to be honest, thoughts of the organ music fill me with some raw spots yet. You'll have to let me think about it."

"Oh, certainly, I wasn't suggesting that—"

"I may seem self-indulgent, but the congregation has adjusted to the piano. And I need to deal with my own problems—and my daughter's—before I deal with someone else's.''

"Yes. Do take your time. I suppose I should have been more considerate in my request.''

"Don't worry about it. How would you know what goes on in my head?''

Mary Beth leaned across the table and latched onto David's arm. "I wish I could help. I'm sure life isn't complete without...well, being alone and with your daughter, too. Hiring a woman to fill in for Nattie's mother is all right, but—''

"Callie is far more than a fill-in. She's a professional nurse, well-trained. I'm very hopeful that her influence with Nattie will bring her out of her cocoon. Callie's full of spirit and a delightful...'' He looked at their astounded faces and realized he had gone overboard in Callie's defense.

Mary Beth stared at him wide-eyed. "Oh, I didn't mean she isn't capable. I'm sure she is. I mean your daughter has needs, but so do—''

"David knows what you meant, Mary Beth,'' John sputtered. "We shouldn't dwell on the subject. Would you care to play a game of Chinese checkers, David?''

Better than the Chinese water torture you're putting me through. David nearly laughed aloud at his thought.

On the first Sunday in March, late in the afternoon, Callie sat curled on the sofa in the library, reading Jane Austen's *Mansfield Park*. She'd read the author's other novels, enjoying the wit and social commentary on the lives of women in the early eighteen-hundreds.

Sometimes, she felt her own life was tangled in social principles.

Today for the first time since her arrival, Callie had gone to church. She had chosen to worship at a new, larger church on Washington Avenue, one with a large vibrant pipe organ. She longed to hear something uplifting, something to take the ache from her heart and give her patience and courage.

Even in church, for the past few years, she had avoided singing. But today she raised her voice, and her spirit lifted with the music. *Sweet hour of prayer, sweet hour of prayer.* Prayer? Had she prayed as she ought to have done? Or had she leaned on her own humble abilities, forgetting God's miracles?

The pastor's voice shot through her mind, like an answer to her question, with the Scripture reading. *"Then you will call upon Me and go and pray to Me, and I will listen to you. And you will seek Me and find Me, when you search for Me, with all your heart."* The morning's message settled into her thoughts. Pray, she must.

Now, as the sun lowered in the sky, Callie snapped on the light. Doing so, a shadow fell across her page. She glanced up to see David standing a distance from her, observing her silently.

He slid into a chair across from her. "Disappointed?"

"Disappointed?"

"With Nattie. I suppose you imagined by now she'd be playing like any six-year-old?" His face told his own story.

"I'm optimistic again. But you're disappointed, I think."

He lowered his head, studying his entwined fingers laying in his lap. "Oh, a little, I suppose. I don't know what to expect, really."

"You can't expect more from her than you do from yourself."

His head shot upward, and Callie swallowed, wondering why she had been so blunt.

"What do you mean?" His brows knit tightly, and his eyes squinted in the artificial light.

Well, here goes. Callie took a deep breath. "You can't hide behind these walls, totally. Not with your business. But look at you. You aren't living, either. Just marking days off the calendar."

"That's what you think, huh?"

"I suppose I'm too forward."

"I expect nothing less."

His eyes, despite the abrupt comment, crinkled in amusement.

"I should be angry at you, but I imagine you're telling the truth."

"That's what I see. Maybe you have another side, but here, everything is shut off. The doors are closed as if you want nothing to escape. Or is it, nothing to enter? You build walls around yourself...or lock yourself in your secret room."

His face pinched again. "Secret room?"

Callie tilted her head forward. "Yes, the room next door. The locked door."

He released a quiet chuckle. "That's my study. I suppose I've gotten into the habit of keeping it locked. All my business secrets are in that room." He rose. "Come. I'll show you."

Callie felt her cheeks grow hot. "No, I didn't mean—"

"Up, up." He reached down and took her hand, pulling her to her feet. "I don't want you to think I have bodies locked away in there or skeletons hiding in the closets."

"I'm sorry. Really."

But her pleading did no good. David wrapped his arm around her shoulder and marched her to the hallway. He turned the handle, and the door opened without a key. He glanced at her with a playful, smug look and pushed open the door.

Though she felt foolish being led in as if she were a naughty child, she savored the warmth of his arm embracing her. She longed to be in his sturdy arms, feeling safe and secure. But as she stepped into the room, he raised his hands to her shoulders and pivoted her in one direction, then the other, showing her the room.

"See. Not one body."

His voice rippled through her. She turned toward him, her eyes begging forgiveness. "I wasn't suggesting you had something bad in here. I meant, you lock yourself away. There's a difference."

He looked deeply into her eyes, and her heart stopped momentarily, dragging her breath from her. When the beat returned, its rhythm galloped through her like a horse and rider traversing rocky ground. Faster. Slower. Faltering. She struggled for control.

"You're right, I suppose," he said.

His words unlocked their gaze. But in the lengthy silence, Callie became flustered. "I'm right?"

"Yes, about locking myself away from the world."

He moved into the room. "Since you're here, come in. As you see, your sitting room is directly above this one. It's the tower room."

The tower intrigued her, and she moved voluntarily into the depth of the uniquely shaped room. The heavy wooden paneling darkened his study in comparison to her sunny room. Centered on one wall, his vast desk faced the outer hall. Tall shelves and a row of file cabinets stood nearby. A leather sofa and chair sat in the center of the room on an elegant Persian carpet.

"All man. No woman's touch here," she said.

A fleeting grin dashed across his face. "This room is mine, remember." His right hand gestured toward the tower room, and she wandered through the archway. Only two windows lit the circular room, smaller then hers above. As she turned, her eyes were drawn to another piano, a console, against an inner wall.

She stepped forward, noticing manuscript paper spread along the stand. She turned to him in surprise. "You write music?"

"Not really."

She felt him withdraw, swiftly rebuilding the wall he had opened when he let her enter his sanctuary. "But this is an unfinished manuscript." Her eyes sought his.

"I used to write music. I haven't touched that in a long time. I haven't played in a long time."

She nodded. Neither had she. She'd let the music in her life die the way part of her had died that terrible day. Yet, today, truth rose from the solemn moment. David would never live again until he lived fully. And neither would she.

A sound caused them to turn toward the foyer. Agnes stood in the doorway of the study.

"Dinner's ready when you are, Mr. Hamilton."

"Fine, we're coming now."

Callie pulled herself from the room. "I'll get Nattie," she said, hurrying into the hallway. She climbed the stairs, trembling over her second revelation of the day. Earlier, she'd considered the importance of prayer. Now, she knew she could ask no one else to join the living unless she lived herself.

After breakfast two weeks later, Callie and Nattie lay together, coloring on the parlor floor. David stepped into the room wearing his overcoat, his briefcase in his hand. He leaned down and kissed Nattie's head. "Goodbye, Nat."

Callie tilted her head and looked at him standing above her. "We'll see you later."

"Yes, I shouldn't be too late. By the way, this Friday I have a meeting in Indianapolis. I don't know if you need to make a trip home, but you're welcome to ride along. The meeting should run only a couple of hours. Perhaps you'd like to visit with your mother."

Callie rose from the floor, surprised at his offer. "Yes, I'd like that. I know my mother would enjoy the visit, and I have a few things I can pick up while I'm there." Retrieving her light-weight clothing excited her more than did visiting with her mother, but she kept that to herself. Most of all she'd enjoy the private time with David. "I'd love to go, if you don't mind."

"Not at all, I'd enjoy the company. And Agnes said she'd be happy to keep an eye on Nattie."

Their gazes connected, and Callie sought the flashing green specks that glinted in his eyes. A flush rose to her neck, and she looked away from him. "I'll call my mother then, so she'll be expecting me."

He nodded and took a step backward toward the door. "Good." He spun around, and she heard the front door close.

Nattie paused momentarily, almost as if she would speak, but instead, she lowered her head and concentrated on her picture. Recently, her dark-toned coloring had given way to brighter shades, one success Callie had noticed. Nattie used a yellow crayon to color the sun, then traded for a medium green to fill in the grass. Big progress in Callie's view.

She stretched out on the floor again next to the child and turned back to her picture: red tulips, green leaves, yellow daffodils. It reminded her that spring lay on their doorstep. Then, without direction, her thoughts jumped to the changing colors in David's eyes. In the morning light that streamed through the window, the colors had shifted and altered, creating earthy, vibrant hues. Her heart skipped at the vision, and the image hummed within her.

Humming. Callie eased back on her elbows and held her breath. She hadn't been humming, but a sweet lilting melody rose to her ears. Without moving, she listened. Softly, Nattie hummed as she concentrated on the coloring book, her silence finally broken.

Callie's pulse raced, and her joy lifted as high as the prayer of thanks she whispered in her mind for the wondrous gift.

Chapter Eight

With David at the wheel, Callie leaned back and enjoyed the passing scenery. Though spring was yet a few days away, a fresh green hue brightened the landscape, and a new warmth promised things to come.

David, too, seemed to sense Nattie's own promise of things to come. Since hearing of her latest progress, David smiled more often. He referred to Callie as another miracle worker, though she reminded him more than once that God worked miracles, she didn't.

David glanced at the dashboard clock. "I figure we'll arrive about eleven. I'll drop you off and still have time to get to the meeting." He shot her a glance. "I should only be a couple of hours."

"Just come when you're finished. I'll be ready I'm sure." She'd probably be ready sooner. Yet she had to admit, she and her mother had plenty to talk about. She had spoken to Grace only briefly since arriving in Bedford.

"Are you sure? Maybe I should call."

Callie opened her shoulder bag and jotted down the telephone number. "Here you go."

"Slip it in my pocket so I remember to take it with me."

She leaned across the space between them, slipping the note into his nearest suit coat pocket. Her fingers tingled at the touch of the soft cashmere wool, and she warmed at his nearness. *Don't get carried away,* she chided herself.

Romantic fantasies had long disappeared from her dreams. She had never known a man before or after the experience of her child's conception. The thought of intimacy with any man frightened her.

As a teen, she had dreamed of the special day when she would dress in a white gown and float down the aisle as a bride, giving herself to a loving man, exploring and learning about love and passion. The dream had vanished as quickly as her virginity, and in its place, shame and guilt festered like an infected wound.

"You're so quiet," David said.

"Sorry. Just thinking."

"I hope they're nice thoughts."

She closed her eyes and avoided the truth. "Yes, they're very nice." She couldn't tell him the private things that filled her mind. No one would ever hear those thoughts. Another reason she could never fall in love.

After a short distance, the outskirts of Indianapolis spread along the horizon, and David soon left her at Grace's front door. She raised her hand as he pulled away, then she entered the house. She expected her mother to be hanging out the window, waiting for her, but instead the rooms were silent.

"Mom," she called. She wandered to the kitchen, where dishes lay piled on the countertop. Very unlike her mother.

"Mother." She listened and heard a noise above her.

"Callie?"

"You're upstairs, I take it." Callie climbed the steps, and saw her mother standing in the hallway, still in her bathrobe. Concern prickled her. Grace never slept late. "What's up with you?"

"I don't know," Grace answered, seeming confused. "I didn't feel well this morning."

"Or last night," Callie added.

"What do you mean?" Grace shuffled down the hallway.

Callie stood by the stairs, transfixed. "The dishes. You didn't clean up after dinner last night. That's not like you at all. Something's wrong. You need to see a doctor."

Grace swished the air with her hand as if erasing her words. "I don't need a doctor. Probably just a little spring cold. You know how they can be."

She studied her mother's face. Grace's mouth was pulled to the side in a faint grimace. Dark circles ringed her eyes, raccoonlike against her pale skin. "I don't know, Mom."

"You go down and make us some coffee, and I'll get dressed. I'll look much better when I wash my face and comb my hair."

Callie moved to her mother's side, giving her a

brief hug. "Okay, but we'll talk about this when you come down."

When she returned to the kitchen, she put on a pot of coffee and rinsed last night's dishes, then loaded the dishwasher. It hadn't been run for a couple of days. Callie's concern was not the untouched dishes or her mother's appearance. Grace loved to play the martyr. Yet today, she denied valiantly that something was wrong. Callie knew something was *very* wrong.

She started the dishwasher, then looked into the refrigerator. "Old Mother Hubbard's cupboard," she said aloud to herself. Inside, she found three eggs and the end of a bread loaf. When the eggs were scrambled and in the frying pan, Callie popped the bread into the toaster. Her mind worked over the problem. No question. Grace wasn't herself. Living two hours away, she'd have to depend on Ken to keep an eye on their mother. She'd call him after breakfast.

Grace entered the kitchen as the toast popped.

"Perfect timing, Mom. I made us some breakfast." Though Callie had eaten, she joined her mother at the table. She heaped the egg on Grace's plate, giving herself only a tablespoon full.

"Now, I'm not going to leave you without knowing what happened. When did you get sick?"

"Please, Callie, I'm fine. Wait until you're an old woman. Then you'll understand about being tired…and confused once in a while." She nibbled the toast.

"I'm tired and confused now, Mom. Age has nothing to do with it. I think you need to see a doctor. You're not ninety. You're only in your mid-sixties. I'll call Ken before I go."

"I felt fine until yesterday afternoon. I got a terrible headache. Sort of achy in my left arm. I think it scared me. I laid down for a while, and it seemed to pass."

Callie pictured the dishes piled on the counter. The problem hadn't passed as fast as Grace wanted her to believe. Rather than press her mother, she allowed Grace to change the subject, and filled her in on Bedford, her progress with Nattie, and a description of the lovely house.

As the time approached to leave, Callie made a doctor's appointment for Grace and phoned Ken. "I know you're busy, but could you please see Mom gets to the doctor?"

"Are you that worried?" Ken asked, sounding as if he thought she was being foolish.

"Look, Ken, she said her arm ached, and she had a bad headache. We can't play around with symptoms. Let's let a doctor tell her it's nothing."

"I suppose you're right."

"And you really should check with her every day or so, at least until she's feeling better."

"Easy for you. You go off and let me do the work, huh?"

"For a change, it won't hurt you. The thought of leaving her here alone bothers me."

"Where's our dear sister Patricia, when we need her?"

Callie sighed at her brother's complaining. "In California, where she's always been. Quit trying to wheedle out of this. Just check on her once in a while. Can you do that?"

"Okay, I give."

Though his voice was teasing, Ken left Callie less

than confident, but there was little else she could do. Before she walked away from the telephone, David called to say he'd be later than expected.

When he finally arrived, Callie hurried out to his car. "Would you mind coming in a minute? Mom insists upon meeting you."

David turned off the ignition and stepped out into the afternoon sunshine, a knowing look etching his face. "We have to make mothers happy."

Callie led him up the porch steps. "I'm worried about her, actually." She glanced at him over her shoulder and grasped the doorknob.

He paused. "Something wrong?"

"Yes, but I'm not sure what. She seems ill, but she denies it."

David's brows furrowed as Callie led him inside. As they came into the living room, Grace eyed him.

"Mother," Callie said, "this is my employer, David Hamilton. David, my mother, Grace Randolph."

David reached forward as if to shake hands, but Grace's arms remained folded against her chest. Unabashed, he retraced his hand and tucked it into his pocket. "I'm sorry to hear you're not feeling well, Mrs. Randolph."

"I'm fine. My daughter lives so far away she's forgotten what I look like."

"Mother," Callie said, controlling her irritation, "you are not fine. I've called Ken, and I want you to promise to call me after you see the doctor."

"It's nothing. You're making a mountain out of nothing."

Callie rested her hand on her mother's shoulder. "Let the doctor tell me that, okay?"

Grace snorted her protest.

"Promise you'll call," Callie said.

After a lengthy pause, Grace nodded her head.

Callie bent and brushed a kiss on her cheek. "We have to go, Mom. Please do as I say."

Callie gave David a desperate look and stepped backward. David proceeded ahead of her and held the door open while Callie gave her mother a final wave, then stepped outside.

When they had settled in the car, Callie rubbed her temples. "She won't call. I'll have to call Ken. I pray he knows something. Sometimes brothers are useless when it comes to asking questions."

David glanced at her. "Do you want to drive up and take her yourself?"

Callie sighed. "I don't know. Ken should be able to handle it. I'll call him when we get home. Maybe I'll feel better."

"That's fine, but if you need to come here, Agnes can keep an eye on Nattie for the day."

"Thanks." She caught his image in the rearview mirror. His concern touched her.

Callie leaned her head against the headrest, and they drove in silence until they passed the city limits of Indianapolis. A few miles beyond the Franklin exit, she straightened in her seat. "Sorry. I'm not good company."

"No problem. Did you get a little rest?"

"Yes, I think I drifted off for a minute. I've spent my life in silent battles with my mother, and now that something's wrong, I'm dealing with some guilt. And a lot of worry."

"That's part of life." David drew his shoulders upward in a deep sigh. "I think we all do that, Callie. It's so easy to take things for granted. Complain and grumble. Then when we're gripped by worry, we have all the 'I wishes' and 'I should haves' thrashing around inside us."

"I want to resolve some of those things with my mom before anything happens. I guess this scare reminded me of that."

"Good. Look at the positive side. And speaking of positive thoughts, how's your stomach? Mine's empty. They only gave us coffee and pastries at the meeting. No good wholesome food. Did you eat at your mother's?"

"I made her breakfast, but I only nibbled."

"Then we'll stop for dinner. We should reach Columbus about five o'clock. I think Weinantz opens about then. The food is excellent. I called Agnes and warned her not to cook for us."

A strange shyness filled her. David had planned ahead for their dinner together. She'd chased such thoughts from her foolish dreams, and now he was making her hopes come true. She could deal with fantasy, but reality made her vulnerable. *The boss is taking his employee to dinner. Nothing more.* She repeated the words over and over in her mind until they reached Columbus.

The town proved to be a surprise. In the middle of small, turn-of-the-century communities, Columbus rose like a contemporary misfit. Buildings of modern design filled the city center; buses carried tourists through the streets to view the renowned architecture. The restaurant lived up to David's praise, and after their meal, Callie relaxed over coffee, the worries of the day softening.

David studied her concerned face, as she sipped from the steaming cup. For the first time since they had left her mother's, a slight smile touched her rosy lips. "You look more relaxed."

"I feel better. The meal was wonderful," Callie said.

Her smile warmed him. "I'm glad. I know what worry can do. And I've had the same guilty thoughts myself. I look at Nattie's situation and blame myself. After Sara's death, I wasn't there for her. Such a little girl, and I crept away like a wounded animal. I feel terrible about that."

"I think it's more than that, David. Something happened. Something more than Sara's death. I don't know exactly what I mean, but her silence seems deeper than normal grief. You know, children are usually known for bouncing back."

"They do." Her comment pushed him deeper into thought. "I don't know. I've always blamed myself." Was she right? What could have happened? Sara's death was no surprise. And still, it hit him harder than he would ever have imagined. Then, what about Nattie? Could something else have happened?

He gazed into Callie's perplexed-looking eyes, and felt his chest tighten. Bluer than the sky. Rich, deep and filled with her own secrets. What dark moments hid behind those lovely eyes?

"What you've been able to do for Nattie makes me so grateful," he said. "You've already made a difference in her life." In *my* life, he thought, feeling his pulse waver as he regarded her. "Nattie leaves her room now...and the humming. Something more will happen. I sense it."

Callie's face tensed. She lowered her eyes, then raised them shyly. "Could we talk a little? About things that might bother you?"

A knot of foreboding formed in his stomach. "Like what?"

"Tell me about Sara's death. You've never said anything, and like I said, I suspect something more happened to Nattie than losing a mother. Was Nattie with Sara when it happened? Would she feel to blame for some reason?"

"To blame? No, how could she?" He closed his eyes for a moment, the awful memories rippling through him. "Sara had cancer. Leukemia. Nattie couldn't feel responsible for that. Anyway, she was only four."

"I know, but children overhear things that they don't understand. They fill in the blanks, make up their own stories, and things get out of context. I just wondered if that might be possible."

"No, I'm sure that didn't happen." Though he said no, thoughts galloped through his mind as he wondered if something had been said to make Nattie feel Sara's death was her fault.

"If she misunderstood something, anything, it might explain her silence," Callie repeated. "I suppose I'm grasping for it all to make sense."

"I've done the same. Wondered. Worried."

"When did you learn your wife had cancer?"

An overwhelming sorrow washed over him, and the answer stuck in his throat. Callie's question disturbed thoughts he'd tucked away. Now they came crashing into his memory. Without knowing, she was treading on raw nerve endings and deep painful wounds that had yet to heal.

Her drawn face overflowed with tenderness. "I'm sorry," she said. "I guess I'm dredging up hurtful memories. I just thought, the more I understand, the more I'll know what to look for."

He reached across the table and touched her hand clasped in a tense fist. At first, she flinched at his touch, but in a heartbeat her hand relaxed.

"You're right. On both counts." He drew his hand away, balling it, too, into a fist. "Sara had leukemia before we married...but we were hopeful. Like all young, idealistic couples, we thought love could solve every problem—even cancer."

"Oh, David, I'm so sorry. I had no idea. And then when she got pregnant..." Callie tossed herself back against the cushion with a lengthy sigh. "Never mind, I understand."

He grimaced. "Thanks." But she didn't really understand. Not everything. He was not ready to open all the wounds. He hid behind her misconceptions in safety. What would she think of him if she knew the whole story? He leaned against the seat and folded his arms across his chest. He had told her enough.

Chapter Nine

The following week Callie stayed in the parlor after dinner, trying to concentrate on her book. Concern dogged her as she assessed Ken's surprise telephone call.

"Dr. Sanders thinks Mom may have had a minor stroke."

"Minor stroke? How bad is that? Major. Minor. The thought scares me, Ken."

"He'll know more after he gets the results of the MRI test. It's scheduled for next week. Apparently, it takes some kind of picture of the brain."

"MRI. Yes, it's magnetic resonance imaging."

"Thank you, Florence."

"Florence? Oh, Nightingale." She snickered. "Poor Florence wouldn't know anything about an MRI. Anyway, how's Mom doing? Do you think I should come up there?"

"She's good. I don't notice a difference."

Callie rolled her eyes. "Do you really think you'd notice?"

"Thanks, sister dear."

"You're welcome. You'll call me as soon as you hear something."

"Don't worry. She's okay...really."

When Callie hung up the receiver, she had a tremendous urge to get in her car and go to Indianapolis. At dinner, she told David. Again, he encouraged her to go if she would feel better, but wisdom stepped in. She'd wait to hear the test results.

After the meal, David went to his study to work, and she relaxed on the sofa, her legs stretched on the cushion and her feet over the edge. Staring at the book propped in her hand, she saw only a blur, as her thoughts twisted and turned. Nattie had carried storybooks down with her before dinner, and she lay on the floor nearby, flipping through the pages.

When David stepped into the room, she and Nattie glanced up.

"Hmm? All the ladies have their noses buried in a book, I see." He walked to Nattie and stroked her hair with his fingers.

Callie watched her raise the book toward her father, and her heart stood still when she heard the child's soft, sweet voice.

"Read to me, Daddy."

"Nattie," David gasped. His eyes widened and his face paled momentarily, then brightened with happiness. "I sure will, sweetheart." He scooped her up in his arms and carried her to the chair.

Callie's heart skipped and hammered in wild rhythm. She fixed on Nattie's face, witnessing the special moment of her first full sentence since her mother's death. Where one sentence lived, there were two. Then three. It was only a matter of time.

Glowing with rapture, David read two storybooks without stopping, holding the child in his arms. She hugged him tightly when he finished, and for the first time, Callie witnessed Nattie showing affection. Callie and David shared the special moment with quiet looks of elation, not wanting to break the spell.

After Nattie had gone to bed, David returned, bounding into the room like a man saved from a firing squad. Callie rose at his exuberant entrance, feeling her own joy. In a flash, he closed the distance between them, grasping her in his arms and pulling her to his chest.

"Thank you. Thank you," he whispered into her hair.

His warmth surrounded her, and the heat of surprise rose to her face.

"What you've brought into our lives has been like a miracle. Two years I've waited and longed for a single sentence, and tonight—" he looked into her eyes "—my prayer was answered."

A gasp escaped her, and David stepped back abruptly as if embarrassed.

"I'm sorry," he said. "I didn't mean to frighten you."

"Surprised me was all. Not frightened." Though she said the words, the truth was that she was shaken by his actions. She hadn't been that close to a man since… She remembered her father's arms comforting her, but that had been so long ago.

"No, I scared you. I saw the look in your face. I'm

sorry. But I didn't think. Tonight's been so wonderful.''

''Oh, David, it is wonderful.'' Though thrilled with the moment, her reaction concerned her. Had she truly been frightened? In her daydreams, she imagined herself in his arms. She had never expected the fantasy to come true. ''I guess I didn't expect—''

''Don't apologize. Any apology should come from me.''

But she didn't hear one. And she didn't want one. Looking into his eyes, she saw a hint of mischief. ''Perhaps,'' Callie teased, ''but I don't hear you apologizing.''

A wry grin lightened his face. ''And you probably won't. It was my way of saying thank you.''

She grinned. ''And much less expensive than a raise.''

While Callie lay in bed that night, thoughts of the evening filtered over her like warm sunshine. Nattie's words, *''Read to me, Daddy,''* sang in Callie's mind like a melody. David's smile and his joy rushed through her, jostling her pulse to a maddening pace. *Stop. I'll never go to sleep.*

Though Callie cautioned herself, she didn't heed her own warning. Again, her thoughts stirred, and she remembered his strong, eager arms embracing her. But with that image, her dreams ended, and her nightmare began.

She stiffened at the thought. What could she do with herself? Frustration dampened her lovely memories, and she threw the pillow over her head, fumbling in her self-inflicted darkness to turn off the lamp.

Her black dreams had lain dormant for weeks. Tonight, like a rolling mist, the nightmare crept silently into her sleep. *As she moved through a fog, a click resounded in her ears. Then, she saw the lock. He flashed his broad, charming smile. "You're nervous enough, I'm sure. We don't want anyone popping in and making things worse, do we?"*

Her chest tightened, anxiety growing inside her. She nodded, afraid to speak.

His fingers ran over the keys in flourished arpeggios, and she lifted her voice, following his fingers, up and down the scales. Her tone sounded pinched in her ears. She wished she could relax so he could hear her natural quality. Suddenly her singing turned to a silent scream.

In the pulsing silence, Callie's eyes opened to blackness. She raised her hand and wiped the perspiration from her hairline. Again she fumbled in the deep darkness for the light switch. The flash of brightness hurt her eyes, and she squinted.

"I can't bear this anymore," she said aloud. "Please, go away and let me live." Her shoulders lifted in a shivered sigh. She pulled her flannel robe over her trembling body and slid her feet into her slippers. Milk? Tea? Something to wash away the dreams.

She dragged herself into the bathroom and rinsed her face. Her image in the mirror frightened her, her skin pale as a gray shroud. She turned from the glass and wandered through her rooms to the hallway. Quietly she edged her way down the stairs. The whole house slept, and falling down a dark staircase would add not only grief to her terrible night, but also chaos to everyone else's rest.

At the bottom of the stairs, the moon shining through the fanlight above the door guided her path around the newel post toward the kitchen. Deeper in the wide foyer, darkness closed in, but she kept the carpet beneath her feet, knowing the door would be straight ahead at the end.

With her hand in front of her, she touched the knob and swung open the door. A light coming from the kitchen surprised her. She hesitated. Having a middle-of-the-night conversation with Agnes didn't appeal to her, but despite the thought, the choice seemed better than turning back.

As she stepped into the kitchen, she halted. It wasn't Agnes, but David, who sat at the table, sipping from a thick mug. When their eyes met, he looked as surprised as she must have. "Well," she said. "I thought I'd be the only nightwalker wandering the house. Am I intruding on your solace?"

"No, to be honest, you're a pleasant sight."

She thought of her ashen face and disheveled hair and grinned. "I beg to differ, but beauty is in the 'beholder's eye,' they say."

His gaze swept hers, and warm tenderness brushed her heart.

"Beauty is," he agreed, and took another drink. He held the cup poised in the air. "How about some hot chocolate?"

The aroma reached her senses. "Sounds wonderful."

"I made more than I wanted. Sit, and I'll get it for you."

He rose and pulled a mug from the cabinet. Callie slid into a chair, running her fingers through her hair and thinking how perfectly terrible she must look.

He poured the cocoa and placed the hot beverage in front of her. "There." He sat again, then regarded her. "So what brings you out of a warm bed in the depths of the night?"

"A mind that won't stop, it seems." She avoided the truth.

"I know what that means. Nattie's in my mind…among other things."

"Business?" she asked, looking into the milk-chocolate liquid. Rays from the overhead light glinted in splayed patterns on the surface of her drink. When she experienced his silence, she looked up. His eyes met hers.

"No, not business. I was thinking about you, to be honest."

Protectively, her hand clutched her robe. "Me? Why?"

He shook his head. "You'll never know how much you mean to me, Callie. All you've done for us here. You're like a breath of spring after a long winter." A grin tugged at the corners of his mouth. "Pretty poetic for the middle of the night, huh?"

She couldn't speak. She struggled to keep her eyes from widening any more than they already had. "But that's why you hired me. To help Nattie."

"But you've done more than that." He reached across the table and laid his hand on hers. "You've helped me, too. I feel alive again, like a man released from prison, his life restored."

Callie looked at his hand pressing against the back of hers. Though her initial thought was to recoil, she joyed in feeling the warm pressure against her skin.

His gaze traced the line of her face. "I wish you'd tell me what troubles you. You know so much about me. I know so little about your life."

She drew her hand from under his and tucked it in her lap. "What troubles me? Nothing really. Old problems crop up once in a while. Nothing you can do about them."

"But...sometimes you seem frightened. Is it me? Are you afraid of me? Callie, I'd never hurt you. If you think—"

Lifting her hand, she pressed her finger on his lips to quiet him. "Please, it's me. Not you."

He raised his hand, capturing her finger against his lips. A kiss as gentle as a fluttering breeze brushed across her skin. Her heart stopped, and she drew in a quick breath. He wrapped her fingers in his and lowered his hand. "I pray someday you can tell me. Whatever it is."

She withdrew her hand a second time. He tilted his head, his face filled with emotion. She wanted to touch his unshaven cheeks with her palms and kiss the worry from his eyes. A worry that she knew was for her, not for himself. Everything in her cried out to tell him, but she pushed the urge deep inside her, praying this time the pangs would stay there.

Patches of sunlight glinted through the sprouting foliage. Callie glanced over her shoulder at Nattie running behind her, looking like any happy child. A rosy glow lit her cheeks, and her eyes sparkled in the brightness of the afternoon.

"Can't keep up with me, can you?" Callie called as she neared the crest of the hill.

Nattie stumbled along, her young, inactive legs not used to the rigors of dashing up a hillside. When Callie reached the top, she fell to the grass, laughing and breathless. Nattie reached her, puffing, and plopped down near her.

Though the hillside was sprinkled with trees, the landscape offered a view of a smattering of houses and distant barns. The new grass and tree leaves, sporting their pale green colors, sent a charge of rebirth and excitement through Callie.

Like spring bursting on the scene, so Nattie's blossoming was another new gift. Nattie had opened her silent world a little more, and brief sentences popped from her like the unexpected surprise of a new Jack-in-the-box. Neither David nor Callie knew at what moment the child might add another sentence to those they had already tallied with joy.

With her heart full of the abounding changes around her, she began with a hum, and before she realized she had risen, as if the trees were her audience, and had opened her mouth in song—*"Beautiful Savior, King of Creation."* She began timidly as a lilting murmur. She hadn't sung in such a long time. But by the third verse, her voice soared into the sky.

Nattie blinked, then widened her curious eyes. A glimmer of awareness covered her face. Callie studied her. Had her mother sung to her in this spot? Or was it the song? Something in the child's look gave Callie a sense of connection. Could music be a catalyst to help the child heal from her terrible hurt?

The sunlight shimmered through Nattie's hair, creating a golden halo around her face. Callie's heart tugged at the lovely picture. Lost forever was the sight of her own child. Since arriving in Bedford, she had locked her own sorrow in her heart's prison. How could she help Nattie if she spent all her energies grieving over something that could never be?

But today, the sorrow gushed from her like a geyser pent up in the earth. Did her child have dark hair like her father, or honey-toned tresses like hers? Were her eyes blue or brown? Was she happy? Or was she sad the way Nattie had been? All the questions that she had stuffed away rose, pouring over her.

She let the questions flow, then, with new conviction, forced them away. In her silence, the only sounds were the chirping birds and a distant mooing cow. Then Nattie tilted her head, and a grin pulled at the corners of her bowed mouth. "Sing more."

Hearing the child's voice, Callie's heart skipped a beat. Her voice little more than a whisper, she asked, "Do you have a favorite?"

Nattie shook her head.

"No favorite?" With a chuckle, Callie leaned down and tickled her neck. "I won't know what to sing for you, then." She sank to the ground as near to Nattie as she dared. "Maybe someday you'll want to sing with me."

Callie began humming softly. A favorite hymn tangled in her memory. As the words unscrambled in her mind, her heart lifted like the melody of the song. *"What wondrous love is this, oh my soul."* The years that her voice had been silenced by her battered memories seemed forgotten. *"That caused the Lord of life to bear the heavy cross."* The child only listened, staring at the ground with an occasional glimpse toward Callie's face. She too bore some secret "heavy cross."

A deep sorrow filled the child's eyes, and when the line of the verse had ended, Callie stopped her song. Music had definitely touched the child's heart. But with *sadness*. Callie longed to tell David her discovery.

Chapter Ten

~⬧

David was out of town again, and Callie felt antsy for adult conversation. With a short grocery list tucked in her shoulder bag, she drove into town. Agnes usually shopped, but today Callie needed fresh air and a distraction, and the housekeeper had graciously agreed to keep an eye on Nattie.

Outside, spring worked its magic on her spirit. She wanted to run and play in the bright, new grass, not be bound to the quiet, closed-in house. She longed to leave her worries and sadness behind.

Through the trees, she caught a glimpse of the steeple of John Spier's church, and an unexplained urge tugged at her. She pulled the car into the empty parking lot, stepped out onto the gravel and looked around. The young pastor's car was parked in the parsonage driveway. She headed for the door, wondering if Pastor John might be working inside.

At the entrance, she pushed the handle on one of the big double doors, and it opened. The bright sunshine spread inside along the worn carpet in the small foyer.

She stepped inside, pulling the weighty door closed. Standing still, she waited for her eyes to adjust to the gloom. She listened for a sound, but heard nothing. With hesitant steps, she wandered down the aisle, which was lit by the daylight shining through the deep-toned stained glass. Above the dark walnut altar hung a large wooden cross. But the image that caught in her eye was the piano.

She moved as if drawn to the fruitwood console, which was flanked by chairs for a small choir. A trembling melancholy clung to her as she edged forward. Her gaze caressed the keys, and she slid onto the bench, an old desire surging within her.

A hymn book lay open on the music stand, and her hands trembled as she placed them on the keyboard. As she followed the music, her fingers felt stiff and uncertain on the keys. Though the grand piano sat in silence at the house, she hadn't been moved to play, perhaps knowing the piano was Sara's.

When the hymn ended, she turned the pages to another, then another. Before she realized it, her voice was lifted in song. *"There's a quiet understanding when we're gathered in the spirit."* She had often sung that song in her church in Indianapolis. Longing tugged at her heart. She had not sung in church for the past seven years, and today, with no congregation, she sang for God alone. When the song ended, she bowed her head.

"That was wonderful."

Callie jumped, her head pivoting at the sound of a familiar voice. "Oh, you scared me."

Pastor John halted. "I'm sorry. I didn't mean to."

"How long were you there?"

Smiling, he shrugged. "About two hymns, I'd say. I didn't want to stop you. You play and sing beautifully."

Her hands slid from the keyboard to her lap. "Thanks. I, um, don't sing much anymore."

"But you should." He leaned toward her, his elbows resting on top of the piano. "You have a real gift. It's a shame not to use it."

Callie's shoulders tensed; she felt cornered. "I...I did years ago."

"We could use a soloist in church some Sundays." He raised his eyebrows in question.

Callie lowered her lids, then raised them. "Yes, well, I've been giving thought to singing again."

"And?"

"And I guess I'm not quite ready."

"Not stage fright? You seem so confidant, I can't imagine your being intimidated by an audience."

His tone pushed her for an explanation. "I don't have stage fright. I had a bad experience a few years ago."

"I'm sorry."

She shifted uncomfortably. "Wounds heal eventually."

"Well, I'll keep your...wound in my prayers."

Callie whispered her thanks, relieved to end the conversation.

John lifted a chair from the choir area and swung it next to the piano. He sat, and a need to escape gripped her. Not wanting to be rude, she struggled against the urge.

He leaned toward her. "Have you ever thought about directing a choir?"

She sputtered a laugh. "Direct? No. Never in my life. I take it you need a choir director."

"Pam Ingram, our pianist, is doing her best, but playing and directing is difficult, especially for someone with limited training."

"Yes, it is." Callie's heart thudded, as she wondered how to escape without being utterly rude. "I really should get going. Agnes is waiting for the groceries." A nervous titter broke from her lips. "Today wasn't the best day to stop, but I've never been here, and…I was curious."

"You're a member somewhere else?"

"No, I've been going to, um, New Hope over on Washington."

John nodded. "Ah, the new church. We have a terrible time keeping members here. They have so much. Including an organ."

Callie's attention was drawn to the small balcony and the line of pipes. "The organ needs work, you mentioned."

"Yes, a few thousand dollars. We don't have it. I'd sort of hoped since Sara Hamilton had been the organist—and David directed the choir—he might make a donation."

Callie's stomach somersaulted. "David was the choir director here?"

His eyebrows shot upward. "Yes, I've been reading all kinds of things to learn the church's history. I was surprised. And so are you, I see."

Callie felt defensive. "He's never mentioned it, but why would he? He's still healing."

"That's what he said."

"So you asked him?"

John rose, stepped to the console, then spun around. "Yes, I mentioned it."

Wounds heal. She prayed they would. Music was the way to reach Nattie. Might David refuse to let her try? Time and patience, that's what they both needed. "Give him time. Things will get better, I'm sure."

A grin curled his lips. "And you? Should I give you time, too, to consider my offer?"

"Your offer?"

"To sing for us? Or help with a choir?"

"Yes, time. It's something we all need." She rose abruptly and stepped to the center aisle before turning around. "I'd better be on my way."

She surveyed the surroundings again as she headed for the door, then stopped halfway down the aisle. "Your church has charm, you know," she said, turning toward him. "New Hope doesn't have charm at all. You should stress that. A lot of people still enjoy the 'old-time religion.'" She waved and rushed up the aisle before he asked her any more questions—or favors.

Though David had returned from his trip, he kept himself closed up in his study. Callie was disappointed. She missed him and hoped to talk to him about the questions that filled her mind regarding Nattie. Sitting in the parlor, she looked through the foyer to the closed door across the way.

Since Nattie had already gone to bed for the night, Callie's responsibilities for the day were over. She rose and marched across the hall, but when she reached the door, she halted. Filling her lungs with air, she released a stream of anxiety from her body, then knocked.

Seconds ticked by. A near-eternity passed before she heard David's response.

"Yes?"

She closed her eyes, prayed, and turned the knob.

David sat at his desk across from the door. "Callie, come in," he said.

She stood shyly near the door. "I'm sorry to disturb you."

"Is something wrong?"

"No, I…I wondered if you have a minute to talk."

"Sure, have a seat." After shuffling the papers in front of him, he rose, motioning for her to sit. "I'm sorry to be hidden away again. I've been preoccupied with a ton of paperwork and some big decisions since I came back from the trip."

"I understand, but I've had a lot on my mind, too." She sank into an overstuffed chair. "And…and I wanted to get your opinion."

David joined her, choosing one of the comfortable chairs across from her. He leaned over with his elbows on his knees, his hands folded in front of him, as he listened to her story of Nattie's day on the hillside. His eyes brightened when he heard about the child's interest in Callie's singing. Yet, as always, sadness followed when he learned of her retreat into silence again.

"But I know music is the key," Callie said. "I believe if I encourage that interest, we'll get somewhere. But since it's a sensitive issue, I wanted to check first. I don't want to do anything that might hurt either of you."

David stared at his shoe, moving the toe along the pattern in the oriental carpet. "I appreciate your concern."

She waited.

In time, he lifted his gaze to hers. "I've been selfish in many ways, protecting myself more than thinking of Nattie." Stress tugged at the corners of his mouth. "I'd like to think I've made some progress. So as they say, you're the nurse. I'll trust your judgment to do what's needed. Anything that will make Nattie a happy child again is fine with me."

Callie relaxed. "Thanks for your confidence."

"You're welcome."

His eyes connected with hers again, and a twinge shot through her chest. The connection sparked liked wires charged with unbound electricity. Finally, she found her voice. "What are you thinking?"

He lowered his gaze. "Nothing. I'm sorry."

She longed to know his thoughts. But she had more to ask, and struggled to organize her musings. "Did Nattie have a particular song she liked to sing with you and Sara?"

David leaned his head back for a moment and then tilted it forward. "Oh, some of the children's songs, I suppose. 'Jesus Loves Me,' for one. Something else about 'two little eyes.'"

"Yes, I know them both. I'll see if she'll sing them with me. I'm grasping for anything."

"Yes, even the slightest progress."

Callie knew she should say good-night, but she longed to be with him, to talk…about anything.

He drifted away in thought. She sensed she should go and leave him with his own reveries, but a playful look glinted in his eyes. "Have you gotten into mischief since I've been gone?"

"Just a little." She grinned. "On the way to town the other day, I stopped by the church. *Your* church, I should say. I talked a bit with Pastor Spier."

"I suppose he's asking you to join the coalition to pry a donation from me."

"No, but he did mention that he'd asked you." She glanced down at her fingers and realized they were tapping the edge of the chair. "He told me you were once the choir director at First Community Church. Is that right?"

David closed his eyes, and lifted his shoulders in a heavy sigh. "Wish I could get my hands on those church records." He peered at her. "Yes, I'm guilty as charged. I did it to help Sara. Playing and directing is difficult. She could do it, but having a director made things easier."

"I just wondered. Was surprised, naturally. But I suppose you have a lot of surprises hidden away that I don't know about."

He flinched. "Only a few. And you seem to pry them out of me daily."

"Good for me." She shifted in her chair. "So, are you thinking about helping with the organ repairs?"

"Should I throw you out on your ear now? Or later?"

A pleasant expression hovered on his face, so she continued. "He paid me good money to pry this information out of you." She rose with a grin. "I'd better leave before you follow through on your threat.'' She headed for the door. ''Good night.''

David rose and stepped toward her. ''How's your mother?''

She spun around, meeting his questioning eyes. ''Mom seems to be fine, but she did have a minor stroke, according to the MRI test. The doctor has her on some new medication. Now all I can do is pray she takes care of herself.''

''I'm glad to hear it was minor. God gives us warnings sometimes, a little reminder to take care of ourselves. Problem is, we have to listen.''

Callie grinned as she turned the doorknob. ''And listening is definitely one of Mom's serious problems.'' She glided through the door and closed it before he could respond.

Climbing the stairs, she hummed a simple children's hymn. The tune brought back old questions. Did her own child, living somewhere in the world, know the song? Had Christian parents adopted her tiny little girl? A heavy ache weighted her heart. Drawn by her emotions, or perhaps more by her loneliness, Callie opened Nattie's bedroom door and tiptoed inside.

The child lay curled in a tiny ball on the edge of her bed. The rosy night-light sent a wash of pink over her face, her cheeks glowing with the warm hue. Callie had fought her instincts so often to lavish her affection on Nattie, knowing it might not be good for the child when she had to leave, and positive it would not be good for her own throbbing hurt.

But tonight, she leaned over, brushed the child's hair from her cheek with her finger, and lay her lips against Nattie's warm, soft skin. Tears filled her eyes as she backed away and turned to the door. Taking one more glimpse, she stepped into the hallway—and into David's arms.

Chapter Eleven

Callie gasped as David held her in his arms outside Nattie's room. Her body trembled in fear as she pulled away from his grasp and closed the bedroom door.

"I didn't mean to frighten you," he said. Pausing, he searched her face, then raised his fingers to capture her chin. "Why do you have tears in your eyes? Is something wrong?"

"Nothing. Nothing's wrong with Nattie, if that's what you mean." Callie released a trembling sigh and pulled herself together.

"But why are you crying?" he whispered, sounding concerned.

"I'm not crying." She kept her eyes lowered, praying the evidence of her tears would vanish. When she raised her eyes to his, he held her riveted.

David lifted his hand and brushed his fingers across her lashes. "Your eyes are still wet. Please tell me what's wrong."

Callie grasped for something to tell him. "I'm worried about my mother, I suppose. Looking down at Nattie reminds me how my mother hovered over me when I was a child. I keep praying for my mother, but fears still creep into my thoughts."

He drew a clean handkerchief from his back pocket and daubed her eyes. "You know, Callie, if you need to go home for a few days, I can manage without you. Not that I want to—but Agnes will take care of Nattie. Please, go home. You'll feel better."

Callie's lie had gotten out of control. She remembered her mother's words that a lie spoken becomes a web of deceit that grows bigger and bigger. "No, really. A good night's sleep is all I need. But thanks for the offer. Maybe one of these days I'll visit her for a weekend."

He rested one hand on her shoulder and tilted her face with the other. "If you're sure?"

His eyes again bound her, and her breath quivered through her body. "I'm sure," she whispered.

His fingers touched her cheek in a tender caress before he pulled his hand away and turned toward his own room.

Callie darted into her bedroom across the hall. Overwhelmed, she shut the door and leaned against the jamb. Her cheek tingled where his fingers had touched, and she raised her own hand and pressed her burning skin.

Her mind raced. Was she a fool? Was his touch only kindness, or had his feelings grown? If he cared about her, she should leave now while she still could. She leaned her head back, pressing her eyelids closed. She could offer him nothing. But how could she walk away from Nattie now that the child had begun to leave her shell.

Foolish. Foolish. Her thoughts were nothing but nonsense. She rushed to the bathroom and turned the shower on to a full, heavy stream, stripping her clothes from her shaking body. She stepped into the tub and let the water rush over her, feeling its calming warmth. She scrubbed herself until her thoughts, like the soapy bubbles, washed down the drain.

No man would love her once he knew the truth. She could offer a man like David nothing but her less-than-perfect self. He deserved a lovely, unsullied woman. She dried herself, rubbing the nubby towel over her body until she glowed bright pink. As she brushed her hair with heavy strokes, she stared at herself in the mirror. No one wanted a used, sinful wife.

Callie tossed the hairbrush on her vanity table and crawled into bed, praying sleep would come quickly. In the darkness, her mind drifted, and, as on so many nights, the mist rolled in. His voice came from the shadows.

"Why, Callie, that's a lovely, lovely name. Nearly pretty as you are, sweetheart."

A flush of excitement deepened to embarrassment. He pulled the door closed behind her, and she stepped inside the room, moving toward the black, gleaming grand piano.

He flashed his broad, charming smile. "You're nervous enough, I'm sure. We don't want anyone popping in and making things worse, do we?" The lock clicked.

Her chest tightened, anxiety growing inside her as

his fingers touched the keys. She wished she could relax, so he could hear her natural quality.

He winked, then eyed her hand resting on the piano edge. He stopped playing and placed his hot, sweaty fingers on hers. "You just relax there. I can hear you have a pretty voice."

Callie filled her diaphragm with air, and her voice soared from her, natural and strong.

He looked at her with admiration, swaying and moving on the bench as she sang. "Why you're a little meadowlark, aren't you."

Callie's eyes shot open in the darkness, as the name pierced the night like a knife, *Meadowlark, Meadowlark.*

A gentle breeze drifted through the open parlor windows. Callie leaned her head against the sofa back, her attention drawn to Nattie. With an array of crayons and a coloring book, Nattie concentrated on her artwork, her golden curls hiding her face. The afternoon sun glinted through the windows, and rays danced on the child's hair like a sprinkle of fairy dust.

Each time Callie allowed herself to think about the little girl, her heart ached. No matter how hard she tried to avoid the inevitable, her heartstrings tangled more and more around Nattie.

Daily, she prayed for Nattie's healing, yet the reality sent a sad shiver through her. Nattie, healthy and happy, would start school in September, and Callie would have completed her task. She would have to leave Bedford. How could she ever say goodbye?

As if the child knew she filled Callie's thoughts, she sat up, tearing the picture carefully from the book.

She rose, glancing with lowered lids toward Callie, then carried the picture to her side.

"How beautiful," Callie said, holding the paper in front of her. "You color so well, Nattie. Everything's inside the lines. And such pretty colors, too. I love it."

Nattie's timid grin brightened her face. "It's for you."

Her pulse skipped a beat, and she clutched the paper to her chest. "Thank you. This is one of the nicest presents I've ever had."

Nattie slid onto the sofa and nestled by her side. Callie pulled herself together, reviewing the event as if it occurred in slow motion. With caution, she slid her arm around the child's shoulders. Nattie leaned into her arm without hesitation. Longing, delight, amazement swirled through her in one rolling surge.

"Oh, Nattie, you are a gem," Callie said.

Nattie tilted her face upward, her brows knit together.

"You don't know what a gem is?"

Nattie shook her head.

"I didn't say a 'germ,' did I?" The moisture in her eyes belied her mirth. "I said a gem. Like a diamond. You know what a diamond is?"

"Uh-huh," Nattie said, her face glowing.

"You're *my* diamond, Nattie."

Nattie snuggled more closely to her side. Callie savored the moment, wishing and longing for miracles, thoughts she couldn't speak for fear of losing them.

The magic moment evaporated when Agnes called them to lunch, but Callie's mind replayed the scene over and over. Nattie had already made a giant stride forward, though Callie had yet to put her plan into effect to use music to draw her out more completely.

The thought filled her mind, and she decided to begin after lunch. When they had settled back in the parlor, Callie wandered to the piano and lifted the bench lid. Inside, she found music books of all kinds. She ruffled through them, pulling out a bound selection of well-known classics. She lowered the lid and adjusted the bench. Nattie watched her with curiosity.

Sliding onto the bench, Callie propped the music on the stand, and glanced through the pages and found a favorite. Her hands rested on the keys covered with the dust of disuse. She made a mental note to clean the ivory with witch hazel. But for now, she allowed her fingers to arch and press the first notes of the sonata.

The rich, vibrant tone of the piano filled the room. Like a tonal magnet, Nattie rose, drawn to the instrument. She stood at Callie's side, her sight riveted to Callie's experienced fingers moving over the keys. The music held the child transfixed, and Callie continued, her emotions caught in the rhythm and tones of the masterpiece.

When she finished the selection, she sought Nattie's eyes. The child's face seemed awed by the experience.

"Would you like to sit next to me?" Callie held her breath.

Nattie tried to scoot onto the bench, and Callie put her arm around the girl's slender shoulders, giving her a boost.

"There, now you can see much better. How about another song?"

Nattie nodded, and Callie selected a shorter piece, hoping to keep the child's interest. The Bach étude resounded in a bright lilting melody, and when she finished, she turned to Nattie. "Okay, now it's your turn. Would you like to play?"

Nattie's eyes widened, and a small grin curved her lips.

"Good. I'll show you a simple song. And later, I'll pick up a beginner's book for you. We can surprise your daddy."

Again, Nattie's quiet voice broke her silence. "Okay."

Though her word was a near whisper, to Callie the sound was a magnificent symphony.

Callie slid the beginner's book into the piano bench when she brought it home from the music store. In her excitement, she wanted to share the moments with David, but she wondered if the fact would stir up sad memories. And she'd only asked him about singing, not piano lessons. Waiting seemed to be the better option. Yet already, Nattie's natural talent blossomed.

She and Nattie had made a pact to keep her lessons a secret. When Nattie felt ready to play for her father, they would hold a surprise concert. Like true comrades, their secret bonded them.

With the music book stowed in its hiding place, Callie returned to her room. Tonight she wanted to give Nattie and David time alone. Each day the child's progress seemed more evident. With more than three months before the beginning of school, Nattie would be ready for first grade.

Bored with television, she turned the clock-radio

dial on her desk. A familiar hymn drifted from the speakers, and the music wrapped around her like a loving arm. She settled into her favorite recliner and leaned back, closing her eyes.

John Spier's request glided into her thoughts. Years had passed since she'd sung in church. But like Nattie, she'd begun to heal. For so long, her throat had knotted when she opened her mouth to sing. Now her voice lifted often in praise to God and in her love of music. Music completed her and made her whole again. At least, almost whole.

Maybe she should consider Pastor John's request. She could praise God all she wanted on the hillside and in private, but singing in church was a loving testimony. Hymns drifted through her mind, favorites she had not sung forever, it seemed.

Woven into the radio's musical offering, Callie heard a rhythmic sound. She lowered the radio's volume. The tap came again. She grinned to herself. The door—someone had knocked. She strode across the room and pulled it open.

David stood outside, a sheepish expression on his face. "We missed you."

Callie stepped backward. "Missed me?"

He scanned her face, then his eyes focused behind her.

Callie turned around and glanced into her sitting room, trying to figure out what he wanted. "Did you want to come in?"

He shifted from one foot to the other. "If you don't mind—I just tucked Nattie in for the night, and I felt lonely."

Callie teetered backward, opening the door for him

to enter. He had never come to visit, and the situation caused her a strange uneasiness. "Have a seat." She motioned to the recliner, but instead, he pulled out a smaller chair from the desk and straddled the seat, resting his hands on the back.

"You're welcome to sit here," she repeated, but he ignored her offer and remained seated. "So." She glanced around her. "I don't have anything to offer you, except tap water." Her nervous titter sounded ridiculous in her ears.

David shook his head. "I didn't come for refreshments. I just wondered why you made yourself so scarce this evening."

"Oh." Callie relaxed. Now she understood. "Well, I thought since Nattie and I spend a lot of quality time together, you and she deserved a night alone. Sometimes, it's nice for the two of you to be together…without me. I'm a distraction."

Again his gaze traced her face. "But a pleasant one," he finally said.

She felt a rush of heat rise to her face, a blush she couldn't hide. "You embarrass me. I don't know how to handle comments like that."

"I suppose that's one of the reasons I find you so lovely."

Her blush deepened. "See, you're doing it again." She covered her face with her hands, feeling like an utter fool.

"You're beautiful when you blush, Callie. You remind me of a butterfly locked in its chamber, then suddenly released." He rested his chin on his arms. "Sorry, my poetry's running wild again."

Her gaze sought his. "But it sounded lovely. Really."

"I can never pay you for the joy you've brought back to my life. Every day I see Nattie grow more open, like the little child she was before her mother died. If it was Sara's death alone or something else that made her so withdrawn, I don't know. But whatever it was, you're bringing her out of it. And I...love you for it. I'm sorry if I've embarrassed you again, but I have to tell you."

Callie's feelings tumbled into words. "I see the same progress. Each day I watch her open up a little more, and I'm happier than I can tell you. But I have to be honest with you. It makes me sad, too."

He studied her. "Sad?"

"When she's herself again, I'm out of a job. Joyful for her. Sad for me. Do you see the paradox? I long to see her bubbling with happiness like children her age—but then I have to say goodbye. And...she's stolen a piece of my heart." Callie lowered her lids, the tears building along her lashes.

David rose, moving to her side in one giant stride. In a flash, he knelt before her and grasped her hand. "No, not goodbye. Nattie needs you...and *will* need you. You're the one who's making her strong again. You can't just up and leave her. Even when she begins school, she'll need support and someone who loves her...a woman who loves her. Little girls need a mother's nurturing, not a father who bungles his way along. Don't even think of leaving us. Please."

Callie heard his words, but what he said knotted in her thoughts. *A mother's nurturing.* By delaying her departure, she would only hurt herself more. Could she bear it? "I appreciate the nice things you're saying. But, David, I have to look after my own well-being, too. Time will tell what I can handle emotionally. I can't make any promises."

"I'm not asking for promises, just understanding that we need you."

Words left her mouth that she didn't bite back fast enough. "What you need, David, is a wife. That's who should be nurturing Nattie, not me. You need to live again, too. I'm sure somewhere in the community is a fine, single woman just waiting to be someone's wife."

To Callie's astonishment, David laughed.

"Please don't laugh at me, David. I'm speaking from my heart."

Again, he touched her hand. "I'm not laughing at you, Callie. Please, don't even think such a thing. I forgot to tell you about our invitation."

"Our invitation?" Her forehead wrinkled to a frown.

"Pastor John called earlier this evening. He asked to speak to you about accompanying him to the church picnic. I told him you had already retired for the evening. Then, Mary Beth latched onto the telephone and invited me."

Callie's stomach flip-flopped with his words. "Pastor John asked me to the picnic?" What she really wanted to say was *"Mary Beth asked you to the picnic?"*

David nodded his head. "Yes, I told him to call you tomorrow. But I couldn't come up with an excuse quick enough, so I had to accept Mary Beth's offer. Please accept John's invitation. At least we can be a buffer for each other. You'll save me from a fate worse than...well, from a trying experience."

Though an unexpected jealousy raged inside her, she contemplated his poignant pleading. A protective camaraderie bound them together. "But accepting the invitation isn't kind, David—not if we're making fun of them."

"I don't mean to make fun. I suppose both of them would be a good—how should I put it—catch. But I'm not ready to be caught, and Mary Beth's efforts are so obvious. I'll have to be honest with her. Somehow."

"Honesty is the best thing."

"Then let me be honest. Make my day worthwhile and accept John's invitation. I can bear it if you're there. And Nattie will want to be with you, too. Please."

She lowered her eyes, and when she raised them, her heart fluttered like the wings of the butterfly David had just compared her to. She nodded.

"Thank you from the bottom of my heart." He rose and stepped back. "I suppose I should let you get back to...whatever you were doing." He turned toward the door.

"David," she said, stopping him in mid-stride. "Could you stay a minute? I'd like to talk."

Chapter Twelve

David faltered when Callie spoke his name. Turning, he faced her, his heart galloping at the sound of her voice. His eyes feasted on her tonight, sitting near him as if she belonged in the house forever. Not an employee, but a woman. A woman who loved his child and who, he prayed, could learn to love him. Startled by his own longings, he shivered.

"I hope I didn't startle you. This has been on my mind for some time now."

He tensed, considering the serious expression on her face. "Is something wrong?"

"No. When I visited the church a while back, Pastor John asked me if I would sing for a Sunday service." She grinned. "He also asked me to direct the choir, but I'll leave that talent to you."

David halted her with a gesture. "Forget that." He wondered if Pastor John had put her up to the comment.

"Well, anyway, I'm thinking about singing, and I wanted to warn you."

"Warn me? You have a lovely voice, Callie. You should sing."

She halted and searched his face. When she spoke, her voice sounded controlled and thoughtful. "How do you know I have a lovely voice?" Her eyes lit with a questioning brightness, as if she'd learned the answer to a secret.

He'd spoken without thinking. "I've heard you sing with Nattie. The children's songs. I have ears."

"And you? Do you sing, David?"

"I sang long ago. Nothing like you."

She squinted as if weighing his response, then continued. "I just wanted to tell you that I'm accepting your pastor's invitation to sing."

"If you're singing—" He faltered over the words. "I'd like to hear you. I'll attend worship that Sunday."

Her eyes widened. "You don't attend worship?"

"I've felt very lonely at First Community. Too many memories." He thought of his promise to Sara. "Since Nattie's doing better, I'm taking her to Sunday School, but I usually drop her off and wait."

"You wait for her." Her eyes widened even more. "David, you'll never get *less* lonely unless you work at it."

But it was more than lonely. Much more. "I'm angry, too, I suppose…at God." The words escaped his control.

"Angry? At God?" Her face bent to a scowl. "Because of Sara's death? But you said you knew she had cancer."

"You've asked a whole parcel of questions. Which do you want me to answer?" Despite the tension edging inside him, a quirky grin flickered on his mouth.

Callie eyed him. "It's wrong, you know, to be angry at God."

"I know." He wandered back to the chair he had left a few minutes earlier and again straddled the seat, leaning on the back. "But as I said before, I had tremendous faith that our love would heal Sara's cancer. A young lover's error. But I had faith. When Sara died, I felt betrayed."

The scowl retreated, and her face overflowed with empathy.

Surprised, he felt his eyes mist at his admission. "And when Nattie reacted like she did, I felt devastated. God took my wife, and then my daughter. I couldn't accept that."

"Oh, David, I understand. We shouldn't, I know, but I've been angry at God, myself. When I stopped singing, I wasn't only punishing my parents, but I probably thought I was hurting God, too."

Her own vulnerability wrapped around his thoughts. Questions that he'd tucked back in his mind surged forward. "And why were you punishing your parents, Callie? What secret hides behind your lovely face?"

She paled, squeezing her saddened eyes closed for a heartbeat. When she opened them, fear clouded her face. "Please don't ask. Don't we all have things in our lives we don't want to talk about to anyone?" She lowered her eyes to her hands knotted in her lap, then raised them and focused on him. "At least, not yet."

David nodded, yet his heart tugged inside; he wanted to know what caused her such pain. What stopped her from sharing her grief with him? What scared her when he touched her? Who had hurt her so badly?

"Thanks for understanding," she added. Her eyes softened as she gazed at him. "I'm pleased Nattie's going to Sunday School."

If he were honest, he couldn't even take credit for that. "I promised Sara I'd raise Nattie to know Jesus. I'm keeping that promise. I take her to Sunday School. But church…my heart hasn't been in it."

"I know you pray, David. Maybe at dinner it's for Nattie, but you do say prayers." Her gaze searched his. "Let's pray for each other, David. Prayers can work miracles. We both need help."

Her eyes glowed with her request as she looked at him. *Prayer.* Such a simple gift he could give her…and himself. "A deal," he said, and rose. "I'll pray for you, and you pray for me. How's that?"

She peered into his eyes. "Not quite what I meant."

Her look penetrated his soul. The guilt he'd hidden under layers of self-pity peeled away, one by one.

"I said, let's pray for each other. 'Where *two* or *three* are gathered,' the Bible says. We need to pray for our *own* needs, too. Still a deal?" Her hand jutted toward him.

He stepped forward and clasped her tiny fingers in his. Their eyes locked as firmly as their handshake, and heat radiated through him like a match flame touched to gasoline, searing his frayed emotions.

He needed her—wanted her in his arms nestled

against him. Yet her fear permeated his thoughts. Moving with caution and tenderness, he drew her to his chest. Her body trembled against him. His voice caught in his throat, and his "thank you" was only a murmur. When he'd corralled his emotions, he gently released her and left the room, feeling as if he had left a piece of his heart behind.

David woke in the morning and looked out the window. The weather couldn't have been better for the church picnic. The sky shone a bright blue, with no hint of rain.

If he hadn't accepted Mary Beth's invitation, he might have looked forward to the occasion, but instead, he glowered as he drove to the parsonage with Callie and Nattie belted in the back seat. He wanted, with all his heart, to seat Callie in the front, but protocol determined the spot belonged to Mary Beth.

When their tedious journey to the park ended, John helped tote their gear, and they found a table beneath a large elm tree.

Nattie clung to Callie's side, her timidity obvious in the crowd of gathering church members. Though distressed at Nattie's discomfort, David found pleasure in watching her relationship with Callie. As soon as she opened a folding chair and sat, Nattie slid onto her lap. The love, evident between them, warmed his heart.

Mary Beth unfolded a chair. "Nattie, aren't you too big to be sitting on your nanny's lap?" Mary Beth asked as she eyed the child. "I think it would be nice if you sat on your own chair here by me." She opened another chair. "I'd like to get to know you better."

Nattie shook her head and Mary Beth's mouth dropped in an awkward gape.

"My, my, aren't we a temperamental child." She plopped into a chair and glowered at Callie, whose protective hand cupped Nattie's shoulder.

"Nattie's shy, Mary Beth," David countered. "Give her time to adjust." He wanted to shake the woman for her comment.

Mary Beth beamed at him with a smile as false as her long, well-polished fingernails. "You're right, David. I wasn't thinking. Let's go for a little walk. What do you say?" She rose without waiting for his response.

David glanced at Callie in desperation, hoping she would intervene. But she only looked at him with an arched eyebrow, and he slumped off, not knowing how to avoid Mary Beth without being rude.

"What did you have in mind?" he asked her, as they moved away from the safe circle of chairs. He realized too late that his question might be misconstrued.

"I'm sorry?" Her pitch elevated.

"I meant, where did you want to walk?"

She let out a minute sigh, her fingers playing with the collar of her blouse. "Nowhere in particular. I thought we might enjoy some privacy."

She had thought wrong, but he allowed her to lead him through the trees and up a grassy knoll. His mind wandered, envisioning Callie and Nattie sitting back under the elm tree.

Mary Beth squeezed his arm. "My, you are quiet today."

Her comment amused him. "Obviously, you don't know me very well. I'm not a live wire, I'm afraid."

His words didn't ruffle her confidence. "You see, then, our little walk is important. We'll get to know each other better."

He shrugged off her statement and uttered a thought of his own. "When are you returning home, Mary Beth?" His blatant question dropped in the air like a cement brick.

His weighted words seemed to squelch her enthusiasm. "I haven't made plans yet. I've considered staying in Bedford for a while. I had hoped to…develop some lasting friendships here."

"I see." *Coward*, David yelled inside his head. How could he tell her with finesse that he didn't want to be one of her lasting friendships. The only friendship he wanted at the moment was Callie. But in her case, he wanted more than friendship.

He tried with discretion to uncurl her fingers from his arm and step away. "I'm sure your brother enjoys your company. And if I recall, the congregation has a number of young women…and men eager for a new friendship. You have a particular young man in mind?"

Her look sought his, sadly pleading, and he wished he could retract his foolish statement, throwing in the white flag. Obviously, she had a man in mind—not a young man, perhaps, but a man. *Him.* "I'm sorry, Mary Beth, my question was much too personal."

She averted her eyes, staring back toward the groups of parishioners gathering under the trees near the pavilion. "I had hoped you already knew the young man I find so attractive."

He pressed his lips together, wondering how to worm his way out of the pitiful situation he'd created. "Sometimes, I'm thick-headed, Mary Beth. My wife's death was two years ago, but I haven't quite thought of myself as single. I've been preoccupied with my daughter's problems. But thanks for your compliment."

Glowing red splotches appeared on her cheeks, and she turned toward their picnic spot beneath the trees off in the distance. "I doubt if anyone will attract your attention until the nanny leaves your employ. You seem to have eyes only for her."

"I beg your pardon?" David might have been less surprised by a kick in the shin. "I don't have a relationship with Callie." *But I want one.* His own realization brought a rush of heat to his neck.

"Your heart does, I think." She turned and headed back toward the picnic tables.

Flustered by her reaction, he followed her. Was his heart that obvious? He could no longer deny his feelings to himself—nor, apparently, to the rest of the world. Perhaps he needed to let Callie in on the news. Or did she know already?

When David walked away with Mary Beth, Callie wished she were the woman on his arm. He had squeezed into her thoughts and into her heart, and she had no way of protecting herself.

A romantic relationship frightened her, even one with David. His innocent touch excited her, yet a prickling of fear crept through her at the thought of intimacy. She had prayed, but had she really given her fear to God?

Callie observed Nattie. The child's gaze, too, followed her father and Mary Beth across the grass. Callie's hand rested lovingly on Nattie's arm, and she brushed the girl's cool, soft skin with her fingers. Her heart swelled, feeling Nattie's body nestled against hers. As David had said, the young girl needed a mother's love, and Callie had so much love to give.

When Callie looked away from Nattie, Pastor John was studying her. Did he see how much she loved the child snuggled in her arm?

"Are you enjoying your life here in Bedford?" he asked. His query sounded innocent, but Callie sensed more behind it.

"Yes, very much."

He nodded with a subtle reflex toward Nattie. "I notice you have other things holding you here, too."

Callie glanced down at the quiet child and back at him. "Pretty obvious, huh?"

"I worry about you. You need to take care of yourself. One day things will change, and you'll be the one left empty-handed. And empty-hearted."

His words washed over her like ice water. "Yes, I know."

"I didn't mean to offend you. I just wish your days could be a little more pleasant for *you*...personally. I'd like to see you if you're willing."

She gave him a blank stare. Obviously, he wasn't referring to church services. Why hadn't she seen this coming? "Well, I've decided to take you up on your Sunday morning offer. I'll be happy to sing occasionally for the worship service."

"Great. I'm pleased to hear that. But...that's not exactly what I had in mind."

"I know, and I'm sorry. For now, let's begin there. I'm not sure how settled I want to get in Bedford. I have family in Indianapolis, and…well, I suppose you understand."

He fixed his eyes to the ground. "For now, then, I'll just enjoy having you sing with us." He lifted his gaze and a half-hearted smile rose to his lips.

"Daddy."

Callie glanced at Nattie, her word a whisper. She looked up to see Mary Beth charging toward them, David following her with a look of helplessness.

Mary Beth shot Callie a glance and plopped into the folding chair. It lurched, giving a precarious bounce to one side. If it hadn't been for John, she might have ended up sitting on the ground.

"Careful," John said, eyeing her and then David. "You could have fallen flat on your face."

She raised her eyes, scanning her audience. "I already have," she sputtered.

Chapter Thirteen

Callie awakened early, knowing this morning she was singing in church. Feeling jittery, she rushed through breakfast and dashed to church before service for a final rehearsal.

Waiting for her solo, she sat in the front row. When the sermon ended, Pastor John gave a faint nod, and she rose and joined the pianist. As the musical introduction to "The Gift of Love" rippled from the keys, Callie faced the congregation.

Already the words of I Corinthians 13 filled her thoughts, *"Faith, hope, and love abide, these three; and the greatest of these is love."* Awareness jolted her. Much of her life had been loveless. Not her childhood, perhaps, but her later years—empty, punishing years of feeling unloved by others, by herself and by God.

As she sang, lifting the words in song, her gaze swept over the congregation. Her stomach tightened. David and Nattie sat conspicuously among them. Two pairs of eyes met hers, and like strands of a fragile cord, woven and bound together, she felt strengthened by their presence. The song touched her heart. What was life without love—both human and divine?

When the service ended, Callie rose and turned to where David and Nattie had been seated, but they were gone. Her pleasure turned to disappointment, and she edged her way to the exit.

As Pastor John greeted the worshipers, he caught Callie's hand before she slipped away and asked her to stay until he was free. She hung in the background, waiting. When the last parishioner had left, he joined her.

"Thanks so much for sharing your wonderful voice with us. And I see you persuaded David to worship with us this morning." He eyed her with a wry smile.

"No, I was as surprised as you."

"Then you've been a good influence without trying."

He made her uneasy. "Perhaps," she said, avoiding his eyes.

"I hope you'll sing again soon."

"Sure. I'll be happy to sing once in a while."

He offered a pleasant nod and rocked back on his heels. "And, by the way," he said, his hand sweeping the breadth of the sanctuary, "we had a few more people here today. Your idea seems to have worked."

She sent her mind back, but came up empty. "My idea?"

"The church with charm, remember? You suggested we advertise we're an old-fashioned church. We hung a few posters in the local supermarkets, and

I put an ad in *The Bedford Bulletin*. I've already noticed a difference.''

"That's great. I'm glad." She sensed he was stall-
ing.

"Well, thanks for the idea." He dug his hands into
his navy blue suit pockets. "And have you given any
thought to *my* idea?"

She felt her brows knit again. "Your idea?"

"That you have dinner with me."

The floor sank beneath her. She kept her eyes connected to his and swallowed. What could she say?
I'm falling in love with my employer.

He shuffled his feet and pulled his hands from his
pockets. His eyes never wavered.

"You know I can't get away easily. Nattie still
needs a lot of—"

"You have a day off? An evening when David's
home?"

She bit the corner of her lip and released it immediately. *Trapped.* "Why don't you call, and I'll
check my schedule."

He contemplated her words for a moment. "All
right, I'll do that." He touched her arm. "Thanks for
singing today."

"You're welcome, John...Pastor John."

"Call me John, Callie."

Callie stepped backward toward the door. "John,
then." She lifted her hand in a wave and hurried
through the door.

When Callie arrived home, David was nowhere in
sight. She climbed the stairs to slip out of her Sunday
clothes. As she approached her room, she noticed

Nattie's door ajar. Listening outside, she heard Nattie singing softly to herself. *"Jesus loves me; this I know."* Her murmured tone was sweet and wispy.

Callie stood still. What might Nattie do if she stepped inside the room? Her heart soared with each note of the song, perfectly in tune. When the melody ceased, she pushed open the door and stood at the threshold.

"Did I hear you singing?" she asked.

Nattie's face sprouted a tiny grin, and she nodded.

"You sing very pretty." Callie took a step forward. "Just like your mom, I would guess."

"Like you," Nattie said.

The child's words danced in her heart. "Thank you." She eyed the scene for a moment. "What are you doing?"

Nattie tilted her head the way David often did. "Playing."

"Playing, huh?" She moved into the room and slid onto the window seat. "I saw you in church. Did you see me?"

Nattie giggled and nodded.

"What's this head nodding? Cat got your tongue?"

Nattie gave another titter, but this time she opened her mouth wide and wiggled her tongue. When she closed her mouth, she added, "You're silly."

"Well, I guess I am."

In one motion, Nattie scurried up from the floor into Callie's arms. Her heart pounding, Callie hugged the child. "Well, what do I owe such a wonderful greeting?"

The child lifted her soft blue eyes to meet hers. "You sang pretty in church."

Air escaped Callie in a fluttered breath. "Thank you, sweetheart. You sounded pretty, too, just now."

The child wrapped her arms around Callie's neck, and Callie drew her to the window seat, keeping her arm around the girl's shoulders. Nattie cuddled to her and laid her head against Callie's side.

"I have an idea. Sometime we can sing together. Maybe on our next walk on the hillside." She glimpsed down at the bright eyes looking up at her. "Okay?"

Nattie nodded, her eyes drooping sleepily.

Callie swung Nattie's legs up on the window seat, and the child rested her head in Callie's lap. With pure joy, Callie caressed the child's cheek and arm as she hummed a lullaby she remembered from her childhood. As the words rose in her mind, she sang them gently, and Nattie's breathing grew deep and steady as she sank into a restful sleep.

She smiled down at the little girl, and when she raised her eyes, David stood in the doorway watching her. Her pulse galloped like a frisky colt in a spring meadow. She longed to rush to his arms.

But then he vanished, and, not wanting to disturb Nattie, Callie eased herself back, leaning her head against the wall. He would have to wait if he'd wanted to talk to her. She was busy being a...mother. The word moved through her like an angel's song, lifting the hairs on her arms.

Later that evening, Callie found a gift-wrapped package next to her dinner plate. She flushed, wondering if John had sent something over in the hopes she would accept his dinner invitation. As she turned the small box over in her hand, David entered the dining room and eased into his chair.

"I wonder where this came from?" Then she saw the look on his face, and knew.

"Just a small token."

A tenderness that filled his eyes caught on her heart strings and, like a kite, tugged and pulled until she let the string go, her love lifting to the sky. "For what?"

"Do you have to ask? I picked it up the other day, and was waiting for the right moment. I saw the perfect moment today. You, with Nattie sleeping on your lap."

"Sorry to ruin the lovely picture, but I don't think Nattie feels well. When I tried to get her ready for dinner, she said she didn't want anything to eat. Her cheeks are a little flushed, too. I'll take her some soup later."

"You can't wiggle out of it, Callie. I saw you holding her in your arms. Please accept my little gift."

She studied the box again, turning it over in her hand. "Thank you. May I open it?"

"Sure, what do you think I'm waiting for?"

She grinned and pulled the tissue from the box. When she lifted the lid, a delicate rosebud lapel pin lay on a cushion of blue velvet. A rosy shade of gold shaped the bud, and the leaves and stem contrasted in the traditional golden hue. "It's beautiful. I've never seen anything like it."

"The clerk told me the pin was designed in one of the Dakotas. Apparently, they're known for three shades of gold. Sorry, this only has two."

She raised her eyes from the lovely brooch, heat

flushing her cheeks. "I do feel deprived. Only two shades of gold, huh?"

"I promise. Your next gift will be three." He locked her in his gaze.

Your next gift. She raised her trembling hand to her heated flesh. "I believe I have two-toned cheeks at the moment."

"I seem to embarrass you, don't I?"

Embarrass? He thrilled her. Her voice bunched in her throat. If she spoke, only a sob would escape. Regaining control of herself, she murmured a simple "thank you."

David rose, and in one stride, stood at her side. He lifted the brooch from the box, unlatched it and pinned it to the wide lapel of Callie's simple summer blouse. "There, now we can eat."

When he sat again, he reached toward her. She glanced at his hand in confusion. But when she saw his bowed head, she lay her icy hand in his, and he asked the blessing. The warmth of his fingers and of his prayer radiated a comforting quiet through her. She whispered her "Amen" with his, then concentrated on dinner, afraid if she thought about anything else, the sentiments of the day might overwhelm her.

As she sat on the wide porch, Callie raised her head from her book at the sound of a car motor. Her stomach tumbled, as Mary Beth stepped from her automobile and crossed to the walk.

"Good morning," she called. "I was passing by and noticed you on the porch. I hope you don't mind that I stopped by."

Callie rose. "No, not at all." If God had wanted

to punish her, he could have zapped her with a bolt of lightning for her lie. Of all the people in the world Callie *didn't* want to see, Mary Beth topped the list.

"Beautiful summer day, isn't it?" Mary Beth commented, flouncing up the porch stairs.

Callie cringed. The woman brought out the worst in her. She summoned her Christian manners. "May I get you some lemonade?"

Mary Beth stood uneasily on the top porch stair. "That would be nice."

"Have a seat," Callie said, pointing to a chair near hers, "and I'll be right back."

She dashed into the house, raced up the stairs, pulled a comb through her hair, smeared lipstick across her lips, then flew down the stairs to the kitchen. Holding her chest, she gasped to Agnes, "A glass of lemonade, please."

Agnes stared at her wide-eyed. "Something wrong?"

"No—yes. Mary Beth Spiers dropped by for a visit."

Agnes didn't seem to understand, but filled a glass with ice cubes and lemonade. "Here you go," she said, handing it to her.

Callie stood a moment to regain her composure, then turned and did her best to saunter back to the porch. Pushing open the screen door, she glued a smile to her face and handed the drink to Mary Beth. Nattie, playing in the yard, glanced at them, but kept her distance.

"The child seems more adjusted now than when I first came to Bedford," Mary Beth said as she eyed Nattie.

"Yes, she is. We thank God every day."

Mary Beth stared at her lemonade, then turned to Callie. "So then, what will you do with yourself?"

"Pardon me?" Callie got the drift of her remark, but she wasn't going to admit a thing.

"I mean, you're a nurse. If the patient is well, the nurse usually finds a new patient, right?" Her eyes widened, and when Callie didn't respond, she blinked. "Wrong?"

"No, for a physical illness, you're right. Nattie's problem is more psychological. Healing is different."

"So you're planning to stay, then?" Her face puckered.

"For a while." Seeing the woman's face caused her to wonder about her own. She struggled to display what she hoped was a pleasant expression. "I'll leave eventually," she added, not wanting to utter the words. "Why do you ask?" Callie already suspected why, but she wanted to hear the woman's explanation.

"Well, uh, I suppose I should be out-and-out honest with you." Her shoulders raised, and she gave a deep, disgruntled sigh. "David is an attractive man, and available. Nattie needs a mother. Someone to give her love and affection. I realize right now that you're providing for her care, but David needs...well—I don't know why I'm explaining this to you."

Callie stared at her in amazement. "I'm not sure why you are, either."

Mary Beth rose, fists clenched at her side. "As long as you're here, David isn't going to realize he needs a wife and a mother for Nattie. I would make him a good companion. You're hired help, Callie. He certainly can't marry his child's nanny, now can he?"

Her words smacked Callie across the face. Struggling for composure, Callie concentrated on keeping her voice level. "I don't think you or I have any business deciding who David should marry." Mary Beth's hand clutched her chest, but Callie continued. "Am I to understand you want me to leave so David will come to his senses and marry you?"

"I didn't say it quite that way. I said, as long as you're here taking care of—"

"Of Nattie. That's what I do here." Callie raised her hand and fondled the two-tone gold rosebud pinned to her summer sweater.

"Well, I wasn't suggesting...I find it very difficult to talk to you."

"If you're waiting for me to leave, I have a piece of advice for you. Don't hold your breath."

Mary Beth's face reddened, and she bolted from her chair. "That's what I get for being honest. If you cared at all for that little girl and her father, you'd feel differently. I'm sorry you don't understand."

She swung on her heel and rushed down the stairs. When she reached the sidewalk, she turned and faced Callie again. "And thank you for the lemonade. It was very good." With that, she spun around and dashed to her car.

Chapter Fourteen

Nattie had made wonderful progress on the piano for a six-year-old. She'd begun her second book in only a few weeks, and Callie listened in awe to her obvious talent. The lessons continued to be their secret, so Nattie practiced during the day when David was at work.

While she practiced, Callie sat nearby, her mind filled with Mary Beth's words. Despite her irritation with the woman, Mary Beth had pinpointed the truth. As long as Callie lived in the house, David wouldn't look for a wife and mother for Nattie.

The image of David falling in love with someone else seeped like poison through Callie's thoughts, making her sick at heart. An inexpressible loneliness surged through her. If she had nothing to offer David, she would be kind to leave. Maybe Mary Beth wasn't the woman for him—but somewhere in the world a lovely young woman waited for a man like David and a beautiful child like Nattie.

Callie pulled herself from her doldrums and eased her way across to the piano, as Nattie finished her piece.

"Was that good?" Her shy eyes sought Callie's.

She rested her hand on Nattie's shoulder. "That was wonderful. Your daddy is going to be so proud of you."

Nattie turned on the bench and faced Callie. "I'm tired of practicing."

"You can stop if you want. You practiced a long time."

She placed her hand in Callie's. "Can we go outside now?"

"Sounds good to me. But first, let's go see what Agnes is doing. I think I smelled cookies earlier."

The child's eyes brightened, and she dragged her tongue across her upper lip. "Yummy. Cookies."

Callie pulled her by the hand. "Let's go see if we can have a sample."

Like two conspirators, they marched toward the kitchen. Agnes, apparently hearing their giggles, waited for them as they came through the door. She placed a plate of cookies on the table, then headed for the cabinet and pulled out two glasses. "Milk goes good with cookies, don't you think?"

"I think you're right, Agnes," Callie said, sliding into a chair next to Nattie.

Before Callie could reach for a cookie, Nattie had one half eaten. Agnes put the glasses of milk on the table, and they munched on cookies and sipped milk until the plate was empty.

"Good thing I only put out a few," Agnes said

with a grin, shaking her finger at them. "You wouldn't have left any for the man of the house."

"My daddy's the man of the house," Nattie announced.

"None other," Callie agreed, tousling her hair. "Thanks, Agnes. They were delicious."

"Thanks, Agnes," Nattie echoed. They rose and headed for the side entrance.

Callie halted at the screen door. "We're going for a walk up on the hill, Agnes. Tell David we'll be back in a while, if he gets home before we do."

The housekeeper nodded, and the screen slammed as they made their way down the steps.

Nattie skipped on ahead, and as she watched from behind, Callie marveled at the change in her. Only months ago, Nattie had been silent and withdrawn. Today she behaved like any six-year-old. Only on occasion did she slip into a deep, thoughtful reverie that filled her young face with dark shadows of sadness. Callie thanked God those times grew fewer and farther apart.

But today, the child skipped on ahead, and only when she reached the highway did she stop and look over her shoulder, waiting for Callie to catch up with her.

Hand in hand, they crossed the street, then raced up the hill and through the trees to their favorite spot, the spot where Nattie had spoken her first words to Callie. Now the fields were overgrown with wildflowers, and wild raspberry bushes bunched together along an unshaded path. Nattie plucked a black-eyed Susan as she twirled through the field, holding it out in front of her to show Callie.

They plopped down to rest under the shade of an elm, where the leaves and sun left speckled patterns on the green grass.

"Can I pick some more flowers? For Daddy."

"You can, but wait until just before we leave, okay? Wildflowers need water. We don't want them to get limp and die before we get them home."

Nattie agreed, then flopped back onto the grass and raised her hand over her head, staring into the cloudy sky. "I can see pictures in the clouds, Callie."

"You can?"

"Uh-huh." She pointed to a large fluffy cumulus.

Callie stretched out on her back next to Nattie, and together they pointed out dragons and elephants and ladies with long hair. The sun spread a warmth over her body, but not as completely as did the glow of her precious moment with Nattie.

As she lay there, Callie's mind filled with old, old songs she remembered her father singing when she was a child. "Buttermilk Sky." "Blue Skies." Then a hymn came to mind, and she sat up cross-legged, humming the tune.

Nattie rolled over on her side and listened for a while in silence, until she touched Callie's leg and said, "Sing."

Callie closed her eyes, and the song filled the air. *"For the beauty of the earth, for the beauty of the skies, for the love which from our birth..."* As Callie sang, Nattie's face glowed. The soft blue of her eyes sparkled with dots of sunshine. If ever in her life Callie had felt fulfilled, today was the day.

Somewhere in the reaches of her mind, the words to the song tumbled out. On the third verse, she rose, lifting her hands to the sky, and Nattie followed her, twirling among the wildflowers.

"For the joy of ear and eye, for the heart and mind's delight."

Then she heard a voice in the distance singing with her, drawing closer. *"For the mystic harmony, linking sense to sound and sight."*

Nattie said the words first. "It's Daddy." She raced from the spot and darted into the grove of trees. Callie stood transfixed for a moment, then thought better and hurried after Nattie. But she had taken only a few steps, when David came through the elms with Nattie in his arms.

A smile filled his face, and as he neared Callie, his rich, resonant baritone voice finished the verse. *"Christ, our Lord to You we raise this our sacrifice of praise."*

When he finished, Nattie giggled in his arms, hugging his neck. "I knew that was you, Daddy."

Callie stood in a daze. "But I didn't."

He unwound Nattie from his arms and slid her to the ground. Then he sank onto a grassy patch, stretching his legs out in front of him. "This is the life."

Callie, still astounded, sank next to him. "You should sing more, David. You talk about me? You have a tremendous voice."

"Not great. Adequate. I can carry a tune."

Callie looked at him and rolled her eyes. "And I gave Sara all the credit for Nattie's talent."

David checked her statement. "We should give God the credit."

Callie stopped in mid-thought. She turned slowly toward him. "You're right." Since the day David had told her about his anger with God, Callie had worried. But his words today eased her mind. And she leaned back on her elbows and breathed in the fresh, sun-warmed air.

David had surprised himself with his comment. But what he said was true. Neither he nor Sara could take credit for Nattie's talent. He'd given the glory to God. He eyed the child, her face glowing and her golden hair curling around her head like a bright halo.

He had an idea, and with a chuckle, he clapped his hands together. "Nattie, pick some daisies for me. With long stems. I'll make something for you."

She dashed off, bringing back a flower on a long spindly stem. "Is this a daisy?"

"That'll do. It's a black-eyed Susan." He pointed to the patch of white flowers nearby. "Those are daisies over there."

She darted away, then hurried back with a couple of the milky-colored blossoms with yellow centers. He sat and wound the stems together, fashioning a daisy chain. Sara had often created flower garlands, but today, as if God had given him another gift, the thought of her didn't press on his heart. Instead, he longed to make a wreath of flowers for Nattie's hair.

As his fingers worked the stems binding the flowers together, he eyed Callie and saw a look of wonderment on her face.

Amazement trickled through him, too, as he pictured himself immersed in blossoms. "I suppose you never thought you'd see the day that I'd sit and make flower garlands, huh?"

She laughed. "No, you're right. Maybe in a hospital for mental therapy—but not sitting here on the grass. Couldn't have imagined it in a million years.''

''See, you just never know.''

Nattie darted back and dropped a few more flowers in his lap, and then headed off again.

''Look at that child, Callie. Can you believe it? I hoped for so long, but I had dark moments when I thought she'd never come out of it. Now here she is— like new.''

''I know. Watching her lifts my spirits higher than anything.''

He raised his eyes to hers. ''I'll tell you what lifts my spirits.''

She sensed what he would say, and her chest tightened in anticipation.

''You. I believe Nattie came around because you've given her the tender love she needs. Not her mother, maybe. But you're soft and gentle like Sara. You're fair, blond hair, blue eyes.''

''Spitting image?''

David shook his head. ''Not spitting,'' he said, giving her an amused grin. ''Only a faint resemblance. And you're a whole different person. Sara was quiet, sometimes too thoughtful. Even before her illness, she concentrated too much on things. She had fun, but…you're full of life and laughter.''

Her face filled with surprise, and for the first time, he realized Callie had no idea how lovely she was.

''When I first met you, the word *spunky* came to mind.''

''Spunky? I always thought I was a bit drab and boring.''

''You?'' David stared at her, amazed. Never in his

life would he think of her as drab and boring. Lively, unpredictable, perhaps a little irritating at times—but never dull and lifeless.

"So what's the grand pause for? You're thinking bad things about me, aren't you?"

Pleasure tumbled through him. "I plead the fifth."

"Swell." She gazed down at the grass and plucked at a blade with her fingers.

"You'll only blush if I tell you what I was thinking. Except for the part about 'irritating.'"

Her head shot upward. "Irritating?" Her brows squeezed together, and she peered at him. "What do you mean 'irritating'?"

"Occasionally."

She arched an eyebrow.

"Once in a while."

She leaned closer, squinting into his teasing eyes.

His heart thundered at their play. "Rarely. Hardly ever. Once in a blue moon." He shrugged. "Okay, never."

She flashed him a bright smile. "See, I knew it."

He felt as if he were sailing into the clouds. He watched Nattie picking daisies, and Callie smiling at him with her glinting, delphinium-blue eyes. He wondered if he'd ever been so content.

When Nattie returned, he rested the daisy chain on her hair and kissed her.

"Am I pretty, Daddy?" She twirled around the way she and Callie had done earlier.

"You're absolutely beautiful."

Her eyes widened. "Like Callie?"

His heart lurched with awareness. "Yes," he murmured, glancing over at the woman who brought unimagined joy to his life. "Just like Callie." He allowed his gaze to sweep over her before he turned back to Nattie. "But we aren't finished here, Nattie. We have another lady who needs a crown."

Nattie regarded Callie with excitement and ran off again, as David's fingers manipulated the stems in his lap.

After a few concentrated minutes, he rested a laurel of flowers on Callie's head, too. Then he rose. "And now, my two princesses, I think we'd better get home. Looking at my sundial, I see Agnes is probably wondering how to keep our dinner warm."

He reached down, extending his hands to Callie. She looked up and took his hands. With one slight pull, she rose as easily as if she were a feather pillow. David smiled at the two most important women in his life, each with sun-speckled hair adorned with a flowered garland.

That night when Callie went to her room, her thoughts drifted back to the three of them in the meadow earlier that day. Each memory brought a warmth to her heart, as she witnessed Nattie stretching herself back into a normal life. But most of all, Callie pictured David, sitting on the grass, weaving flowers into crowns for their hair. She chuckled to herself, remembering the day they had met and his stern, pinched face.

Yet her joy changed to apprehension when she thought about the future. For them, she saw no hope of a life together. Mary Beth had planted a seed in her mind that continued to grow. When September came, whether she wanted to or not, she must leave.

Going home would be the best for David and for Callie. Though she'd warned herself many times, she had done the unthinkable. She had fallen in love with him.

At first, she wondered if her love for Nattie had made her think fondly of David. Yet the more time she spent with him, the more she was sure that wasn't true. She loved him as a man, not as Nattie's father. He excited her. His touch thrilled her.

Yet her old fears crept into her mind when she least wanted them to. Like her haunting dreams, they covered her with empty, hopeless thoughts.

She rose and turned on the lamp in her bedroom. A shower would relax her, and maybe she could sleep. She turned the nozzle on full blast and stepped into the steaming water, letting it wash over her and soothe her tightened muscles. Afterwards, when dry, she massaged her skin with the vanilla-and-spice-scented cream that reminded her of Agnes's cookies. Her stomach growled, and she chuckled to herself.

Slipping her feet beneath the blankets, Callie fluffed her pillow and snapped off the light. Behind her eyelids, she saw again the afternoon sky filled with puffy white clouds: animals, people and wonderful imaginary shapes.

Then David appeared, lifting a garland of flowers and resting it on her head. In her imagination, his hands touched her face tenderly and his arms reached out, pulling her to him.

But then as sleep descended, the clouds, too, lowered, turning to a gray, swirling mist, and Callie heard the *click* of a lock. The black dream enveloped her, and David's handsome face changed into the face leering from the shadows.

He winked and placed his hot hand on hers. "You just relax there. I can hear you have a pretty voice. Take a nice deep breath. Throw out your chest and fill those lungs."

She drew a deep breath, her blouse buttons pulling against the cloth as her lungs expanded and her diaphragm stretched.

"That's better." He smiled, gazing at her with admiration.

But when she saw his eyes resting on the gaping buttons, the air shot from her.

His fingers moved across the keys, his body swaying on the bench, as she sang. When he played the final cord, his hands rose immediately into applause. "Why, you're a little meadowlark, aren't you?"

He rose and beckoned her with a finger to a sofa across the room. "Have a seat here so we can talk." She froze in place, his leering eyes riveting her to the floor, and as he reached toward her, a soundless scream rose in her throat.

Callie opened her eyes, her body trembling as she stared into the darkness. *It's only the dream. I'm dreaming.* She wiped the perspiration from her brow and rolled over on her side. Someday the dream would fade. It had to.

Chapter Fifteen

"Well, what do you think?" Callie asked, as Nattie grinned from the piano bench. "Is tonight our surprise concert?"

Her golden curls bounced in the sunlight streaming through the windows. "Uh-huh," she said, giving a nod, "and we'll really surprise him, too."

"We sure will. You play so well already, Nat. I'm proud of you." She rose from the chair and gave the child a squeeze. "Right after dinner, we'll tell him to come into the parlor. Then, I'll be the announcer, and you stand up and take a bow."

Nattie giggled, as Callie described the scene. Filled with their conspiracy, they tiptoed from the parlor and raced up the stairs to wait for David to come home.

They filled their time with puzzles and a storybook, until a car door slam alerted them.

"Daddy's home," Nattie said, peering out the window and turning to Callie with her hand over her mouth to suppress her giggle.

"I heard, but don't forget, we can't let on about the secret."

"Okay," she said, a mischievous twinkle in her eye.

Shortly, his footsteps reverberated on the stairs, and Nattie jumped up and raced to the doorway. "Daddy." She lurched into his arms.

As she did daily, Callie watched their reunion. Since Nattie's return from her quiet world, their day had established a few pleasant routines. At the sound of David's arrival, Nattie dropped whatever she was doing to greet him. Best of all, David's love, once shrouded by his own knotted emotions, had opened as widely as his arms now stretching toward his daughter.

With Nattie captured in his embrace, he looked at Callie over her shoulder. "So what have the two of you been up to, today?"

Nattie let out a giggle and glanced at Callie.

Without giving away their secret, Callie shushed her with a look, then said to David, "Just our usual fun-filled day. Nothing special—puzzles, storybooks, the usual." She figured "the usual" covered the piano practice.

David eased Nattie to the floor. "Well, I think I'll change. Agnes said dinner's in a half-hour."

"We'll see you there," Callie said, grasping Nattie's hand and pulling her back into her room before she burst with the news.

Callie tempered Nattie's excitement at dinner. But as the evening progressed, the child's gaze lingered on her, beseeching her to conclude the meal so the surprise concert could begin.

David, for a change, filled the time with talk about some new business opportunities. Rarely did he bring his work to the table, but tonight Callie listened with appreciation, knowing that the chatter distracted Nattie from blurting their after-dinner plans.

"I have an idea," Callie suggested. "Let's have dessert in the parlor a little later. Agnes made home-made peach pie, and I suspect we all need to rest our stomachs before dessert."

"Sounds good to me," David said, folding his napkin and dropping it alongside his plate. He slid back his chair and rose. "How about you, Nat? Willing to wait for dessert?"

She eyed Callie before she commented. "Yes, because I want to show you something now."

"Show me something? Hmm? What could it be? A picture?"

Nattie jumped from her chair. "Nope. Come on, Daddy, and I'll show you our surprise."

David glanced at Callie. She only shrugged innocently. But when he turned his back, she gave Nattie a wink. The child giggled and skipped off to the parlor.

Callie expected to find Nattie seated at the piano when they caught up with her, but she had remembered their plan and now waited in a chair, her hands folded in her lap. Callie delighted in the heartwarming picture.

"So where's my surprise?" David asked as he entered the room.

"Don't rush us," Callie cautioned. "You sit down right there." She pointed to the chair in good view of the piano. "Are you ready?"

He looked at her, a confused frown knitting his brows. "As ready as I'll ever be."

"Okay, then, let me introduce our entertainment for the evening. Da-da-da-dum!" Callie imitated a drumroll. "Give a warm welcome to Nattie Hamilton, who will perform for us on the grand piano." She began the applause.

David gaped and looked at Nattie, who rose from her chair, bowed and scurried to the piano.

She grinned at her father, then slid a book from under the seat and propped it on the music stand. Easing onto the bench, she adjusted the music book, arched her fingers over the keys and began the song she had prepared: Bach's étude, "Minuet." Her small fingers struck the keys, sending the spirited melody dancing across the room.

With his mouth hanging open like a Venus flytrap, David's attention was riveted on his daughter. When she struck the final note, his quick look at Callie's amused expression prompted him to snap his mouth closed with embarrassment.

Callie burst into applause, praying that David wasn't angry. But in a heartbeat, his surprised expression turned to joy, and he leaped from the chair in a thundering ovation and a cry of "Bravo!"

Nattie slipped from the piano bench, pulled out her pant legs as if she wore a skirt, and took a deep bow.

He bolted to her side and knelt to embrace her. "Oh, Nat, I'm so proud of you. Just like your mom." Turning, his eyes focused on Callie, who was standing in the distance and observing the scene. "And I know I have you to thank for her lessons."

She lowered her lids to hide the tender tears that rose in her eyes. "You're welcome."

"Nat, this is the best concert I've ever heard. You are my personal star."

Nattie grinned and wrapped her arms around his neck. "I'm your star."

"You sure are. Best gift in the whole world." He rose, taking one of her hands. "So when have you been practicing?"

"Every day," Nattie told him. "After you go to work. But we couldn't practice on Saturdays or Sundays. Otherwise, you'd hear me. I'm on my third book already."

David turned to Callie. "You've been buying her music books?"

She nodded.

"You are a gem, Callie. A real gem."

"She's a diamond, just like me." Nattie's voice burst with excitement. "Callie told me I was her gem. Did you know that means a 'diamond,' Daddy?"

David raised his hand quickly and wiped what Callie guessed was a tear that had escaped his eye. "I do. You're both my diamonds."

Nattie ran to Callie's side, hugging her waist. "We're Daddy's diamonds, Callie."

She looked down at the child's beaming face. "I heard. That makes us both pretty special."

"Yep," she said, her head resting against Callie's hip.

Callie looked at David. "Before our throats are too knotted to enjoy dessert, I should probably ask Agnes to bring in the pie. What do you say?"

He grinned, his eyes glistening with moisture. "I

say, you're not only a diamond, but a very wise woman."

When John Spier called, Callie could think of no excuse. She agreed to attend a jazz concert at the historic Opera House in Mitchell. When she accepted the invitation, he suggested dinner, as well.

A whole evening with John didn't excite her. But she'd told him to call, and he'd done what she asked.

Telling David was difficult. She had no idea whether he cared or not, but *she* cared. And she took forever to harness her courage.

"Tonight?" David asked.

"Yes." She wanted to tell him she'd rather stay home and sit in the parlor with him, but her truthfulness would only embarrass her, and lead nowhere. "But if it's a problem, I'll call him and explain. I didn't give you much notice."

"No, that's fine, Callie. I, ah…I have no plans for the evening."

Disappointment filled her. She wished, at least, that he looked upset or inconvenienced.

He peered at his shoes. "You need a private life. You devote a lot of time to us."

"All right, if you don't mind." She had so much more to say—but if he didn't care, why should she? "I'll go, then. Thank you."

"You're welcome," he said, glancing at her. "Have a nice time."

Suddenly her disappointment turned to irritation. "I'm sure I will," she said, her voice picking up a spark. "I'll go."

"Good."

This time his tone sounded edgy. She turned and left the study. Nattie stood in the hallway, peering at her, as Callie came from the room. She had more than two hours to get ready, but she wasn't going to sit there and feel sorry for herself. She had a date, and she'd enjoy herself if it killed her.

With a final look at David through the doorway, she charged up the stairs and into her room. Plopping on the edge of her bed, she stared into her open closet. What should she wear? Hardly anything she owned seemed appropriate for a date. She needed to go on a shopping spree—but where around here? Shopping meant a trip to Indianapolis. More guilt rose as she thought of her mother.

Though they talked on the telephone, Callie hadn't been home to visit Grace in a while. She should arrange a trip. *Trip?* In September, she would be leaving Bedford altogether. Bleak dread raked through her. But it was a cold, hard fact.

She rose and maneuvered her outfits along the wooden rod, glancing at skirts, blouses, dresses. The Opera House. Was it dressy? She was positive she didn't have anything appropriate. Taking care of Nattie didn't require fancy dress, only casual. She searched through the clothing again, but stopped when she heard a noise at the hall door.

She turned and saw Nattie peering in from the sitting room. "Come in, Nat."

Nattie rarely came to Callie's room, and today she edged through the door.

"Did you need something?"

Nattie shook her head, her eyes focused on the closet. "Are you going away?" she asked.

"Uh-huh," Callie said, peering at a summery dress she held in front of her on the hanger.

"Please, don't go away." Nattie's voice quivered with emotion.

Callie spun around and faced her. Nattie's lower lip trembled, leaving Callie confused. "What's wrong? Don't you feel well?"

She shook her head. "I don't want you to leave. Who will take care of me?"

Callie crossed to her and knelt to hold her. "No, I'm not leaving for good. Just for tonight, Nat. Your daddy's home, and Agnes. They'll be here. I'll be back later."

Nattie's misty eyes widened. "Oh...I thought you were going away."

"What would make you say that? Heaven forbid. I wouldn't leave you." Nattie lay her head on Callie's shoulder, and the unintended lie she had uttered, like a boomerang, spun back, whacking her conscience. Hadn't she just decided she would leave Bedford in September?

She gazed into the child's sad face and couldn't bring herself to say any more. Instead, she held Nattie tightly to her chest until she felt her relax, then tickled her under the chin. "So, you thought I was leaving you. You silly. Wouldn't I tell you if I were going away for good?"

"But you and Daddy hollered. I thought—"

"No, we were just talking loudly. There's a difference. And don't you worry about that, anyway. I'm not going anywhere, except out to dinner and to a concert with Pastor John."

Nattie tilted her head, staring directly into her eyes. "Why don't you go with Daddy?"

The child's look of sincerity tugged at Callie's heartstrings. Yet, the words made her smile. Sometimes she wondered the same thing. What might it be like to spend an evening with David—on a real date? She took a minute to find her voice. "I suppose because your daddy didn't ask me—"

"Didn't ask you what?"

Her head shot upward, and she felt a flush spill over her face like a can of rose-colored paint. "I didn't hear you."

David stepped into the room. "Yes, I know. So what didn't I ask you?"

"You didn't ask Callie to go to dinner," Nattie offered, still hugging Callie's neck.

"And why would I do that?" He glowered at Callie.

She unleashed Nattie's arms, then rose. "You shouldn't. She's upset because she thought I was leaving—for good. I explained I was going out with John."

"Ah," David said. "She thought that because you were yelling at me."

Callie lifted her chin. "*I* yelled at *you?*"

"Yes. And now she wants to know why I don't take you to dinner and the concert?"

Nattie shook her head, her eyes wide, certainly not understanding all the innuendos.

Callie glared at him. "Yes, that's what she asked." She waited for his arrogant, stinging response.

"I guess," he said, kneeling down to Nattie, "that I didn't think of it first."

Callie's mouth dropped open wider than David's had days earlier at Nattie's concert. Her pulsed raced like an *arpeggio*.

He raised his soft, apologizing eyes to hers, and she faltered backward, grasping the dresser to steady her trembling legs. "You've caught me off guard."

His full, parted lips flickered to a smile. "Yes, I see that. You can close your mouth now." He scooped Nattie into his arms, as she let out a squeal. "We'd better let Miss Randolph get herself decked out for her *date*, Nattie."

"Who's Miss Randolph?" Nattie asked, as he carried her, giggling, toward the door.

He glanced at Callie over his shoulder. "I'm not sure myself, Nattie. I have to figure that one out."

Chapter Sixteen

When Callie arrived home from her evening with John, David's study light glowed through the tower room window. She said good-night to John and hurried inside. Stopping outside the study door, she paused. She longed to talk to him, but couldn't bolster her courage, so instead she headed upstairs to her room.

The evening had been a strange one. She wondered if, instead of being interested in her, after all, he hoped she could be a liaison between David and the church. Though John said how much he enjoyed her company, the conversation continued to backtrack to the church, the broken organ, and a variety of other congregational concerns.

Callie had decided a pastor's life must be a difficult one, and her heart softened a little as she'd listened to him. She knew the pianist was leaving, and he needed a replacement or, at least, a substitute until a new pianist could be found. Callie sat beside him feeling guilty. He knew she played the piano, and by the end of the evening, she suggested that she might consider helping out ''in a pinch.''

As well as addressing John's concerns, Callie had her own. She couldn't get Nattie's question out of her mind: *''Are you going away?''* Thinking of the situation, she ached. It was no-win. If she stayed with Nattie, David would eventually fall in love and find a wife. She didn't know if she could bear it.

Still, she knew David's feelings for her had grown. At the thought, her heart soared—until reality smacked her in the face and her feelings nosedived to the ground. How many times did she have to tell herself she had nothing to offer him? She could never allow him to fall in love with her—nor she with him.

With her mind in a turmoil, she climbed into bed. She lay for a long time, her thoughts pacing back and forth like someone waiting for a last meal. She knew she was a loser no matter how she looked at it—and was suffering because her actions would also hurt Nattie.

Finally her eyes grew heavy, and she drifted to a near sleep, awakened again, then succumbed. And as her mind glided into sleep, so the shadows rose from her subconscious.

With his hot hand on hers, she heard him. ''You just relax there, little lady. I can hear you have a pretty voice. Take a nice deep breath. Throw out your chest and fill those lungs.''

She drew a deep breath, her blouse buttons pulling against the cloth, and she saw his eyes resting on the gaping buttons.

''That's better.'' He smiled. ''Let's try a song.

We'll do one you know." He handed her some sheet music. "Pick something you know well."

She made her selection and handed him the music. She heard the introduction clearly and filled her diaphragm with air. She opened her mouth, and her pure, natural voice, filled with strength and joy, soared from her.

He gazed at her with admiration, swaying on the bench, as she sang. When he played the final cord, his hands rose immediately into applause. "Why you're a little meadowlark, aren't you."

He rose, beckoning her to follow him across the room to the sofa. "Have a seat, my little Meadowlark, so we can talk business. Her heart raced at first, then the hammering began. He settled next to her, placing his hand on hers. "Are you more comfortable now?"

"Yes," she said, trying to extract her hand. "A little nervous, I guess."

"How old are you?"

"Just turned nineteen. I'm a sophomore at the University of Indiana."

"You'd really like to sing with our group, wouldn't you? Travel with us in the summer? I'm sure you'd be grateful for a place in our choir."

"Oh, I would. Yes, my father thinks you're wonderful."

"And you? Am I wonderful, Meadowlark?"

His hand slid across her knee, and she grabbed it, holding him back. But his strength overpowered her.

"You want to make your daddy proud, don't you? If you want your daddy to be proud, you have to please me a little. How about a kiss?"

His face loomed above her. Her chest hammered,

*thundered inside her, and she opened her mouth to
scream, but she had no voice. Instead, she couldn't
breathe, she was sinking into some deep swirling
ocean of icy black water. She heard her blouse tearing and felt her skirt rising on her thighs, and she
died beneath the blackness.*

When Callie woke, her hands clasped the blankets
and her arms ached from fighting off the monster in
her dream. She had kept her secret from everyone.
No one knew why she had stopped singing. No one
knew what had happened—only she and Jim McKee.

She rolled on her side and snapped on the light,
squinting at the brightness. Why had she not pulled
herself from the dream sooner? Lately, she'd been
able to stop the dream before the end, but tonight the
horrible memory wrenched through her. All the filth
and pain she had felt these past years lay on her
shoulders.

Callie rose from her bed and went into the bathroom, ran cool tap water over her face and arms. She
returned to the bedroom and eased herself to the edge
of the bed, noticing the clock. Only twenty-five
minutes had passed since she'd crawled under the
sheets. She needed to talk to David, to do something
to make the terrible thoughts go away. But if she
talked tonight, she might regret it. The burden she had
carried so many years struggled for release.

She leaned back again on the pillow and dimmed
the bulb to a soft glow. As she folded her hands behind her head, her mind wandered, and while it
strayed, she heard faintly, a soft, lilting melody drift
through the room. Her radio? Had she accidentally set
the clock-radio alarm?

She rose and strode to the sitting room. The sound was stronger there, louder than in her bedroom. Television? A recording? She listened more closely. A piano coming from below. Was David playing the piano? She had never heard him play. The music rose through the walls, poignant and beautiful.

She slipped into sweatpants and shirt, and opened her sitting room door. The hallway was empty. No light glowed beneath the second-floor doorways. She followed the stairs down to the dimly lit foyer. A light still shone beneath David's study door, and from outside, she heard the lovely, haunting melody.

Whether wise or not, she turned the knob and eased the door open. Barefoot, she tiptoed into the room, following the music coming from the piano. As she reached the archway, she stood back and watched David's shadow dip and bend as his body moved with the rapture of the music. Her heart soared, yet wept at the haunting sound.

When the last strain died away, he sat with his head bowed, then, as if he sensed her presence, he turned. She stepped through the opening, and his gaze lifted to her face, caressing her, his eyes glistening with emotion.

"Callie, I thought you were sleeping." He rose and moved toward her. "Is something wrong? Did I wake you?"

"No. A dream woke me." She closed the distance between them. "David, the song was beautiful. What is it?" She glanced toward the piano and saw his manuscript spread out on the music stand. "You wrote that, David?" Callie dashed to the paper and lifted the music. "You wrote this." She swung to face him.

He rested his hands on her shoulders. "Yes, I wrote it. It's been playing in my mind for months, but I hadn't written in so long, not since...since Sara died. I didn't think I'd write again. But I couldn't make the music stop roaring in my head until I put it on paper."

Swirling emotion drew her eyes to his, and in them, she searched for an answer. His words promised a release for her. He couldn't make the music stop until he put it on paper. Would her dreams stop if she said them aloud?

She struggled with her thoughts. The truth lay in his heart and in hers. If he knew, could he love her? If she told him, would she be released from her self-made prison? Could she take the chance? She slid the music back on the stand.

"Callie, I could no more fight the music in my head than I can fight the feelings inside me. You should know that I love you. I've been falling in love with you ever since the day we met."

"Oh, please, David, don't say anything that will hurt us."

"Hurt you? Never. My feelings are far too powerful to hide any longer. I've tried to sense how you feel about me. I'd hoped you were learning to love me, too."

"There are too many things you don't know about me, David. Awful things. If you knew them, you wouldn't say you loved me. I've struggled with them in my dreams, but not aloud. They hurt too bad. Please, don't say you love me."

David looked into her eyes, trying to fathom what

terrible things she could mean. Her eyes glowed, but with fear. He felt her trepidation in the tension of her shoulders. He drew her to him and wrapped his arms around her.

"Please, Callie, tell me. Do you love me? If you love me, I can handle anything. Whatever you need to tell me. I promise."

She clung rigidly to his arms, and he sensed her panic.

"Don't promise anything until you know the truth," she pleaded. "I couldn't bear to have you reject me."

"Then you do love me? Say it, please."

"I've tried not to love you. For a long time, I told myself I only loved Nattie, but I can't lie. Yes, I do love you, but I can never marry you…or anyone. Never."

He caught her face in his hands and lowered his lips to hers. Her mouth yielded to his, but just as quickly, she pulled away. Instead, he kissed her cheeks and her eyes, tasting the saltiness of the tears that clung to her lashes.

"Callie, if you love me, you'll tell me what's wrong. Let me know what's hurt you so badly. Maybe I can help you."

"Please, let me think about it, David. Play your music for me again. I'd love to hear your song once more. I'll sit right here." She backed up and lowered herself into a chair.

"Promise you'll tell me?"

"I promise I'll think about it."

"Promise you'll tell me, Callie."

"Play for me, David, and I'll try."

David looked with longing into her eyes, and didn't argue, but wandered to the piano and slid onto the bench, shifting the music on the stand. He glanced at her, then lifted his eyes to the music. He played, and the love he'd felt for these past months rose from the keys and drifted through the room.

He sensed her watching him, and he trembled at the thought. As his attention drifted to the last phrase of music, she rose and moved across the floor to stand behind him, her hands resting on his shoulders. He felt the warmth of her hands on his arms, and his fingers tingled with the fire burning in his heart.

On the last chord, he turned to her, and tears ran down her cheeks. Her eyes were focused on the sheet of music resting on the stand. Almost imperceptibly, he heard her whisper, "'Callie's Song.' You named it for me."

He swiveled on the bench. "The music is you, Callie. All the longing and joy, fear, confusion, wonder you brought into our lives here. Nattie, you, me, everything."

She stared at him in disbelief. "Thank you," she whispered.

He stood and placed his hands on her arms. "Thanks to you, Callie." He took her hand and led her toward the door. "Let's sit in the parlor. It's more comfortable there. We need to talk. I'll make us a cup of tea. How does that sound?"

She nodded and followed him, his arm guiding her. When they reached the foyer, he kissed her cheek, aiming her into the parlor as he turned toward the kitchen.

Callie wandered through the doorway, wondering

what she would do now. Where could she begin? She had so much she should tell him, yet so little she wanted to admit. He loved her. And she had finally told him the truth: she loved him with all her heart. And Nattie, too. But...

She eased herself onto the sofa, her gaze sweeping the room. The grand piano stood in silence in the bay window, and she thought about the wonderful day, not long ago, when Nattie had played her concert. What happiness she had felt that day. But tonight, though David's song touched her with tenderness, her pulse tripped in fear at the story David wanted her to tell.

Hearing his steps in the foyer, she looked toward the doorway. He came into the room carrying two mugs, and sending a steamy, fragrant mist into the air. Handing one mug to her, he sat by her side, stretching his legs in front of him. "Be careful. This stuff's really hot."

She blew on the beverage before taking a cautious sip, and curled her legs underneath her.

David studied her. "So. Where do we begin?"

She stared at her hands folded in her lap. "I was trying to decide while you were getting the tea. This is very difficult for me. Harder than you can ever imagine. If I get through this, David, you should know you're the only person in the whole world I've told this to."

"I know. You've suffered far too long for whatever this is about. I'm honored to be the one you trust enough to tell."

A sigh tore through her, and an unbelievable desperation raged inside. A sob escaped from her throat. She swallowed it back, choking on the emotion.

He took her hand in his and brushed her skin with his fingertips without speaking.

Another sigh rattled from her. With a gentle touch, David caressed her hand. Then she began, slowly at first.

"Seven years ago I sang in church, in college—anywhere an audience would listen. I studied music in college. Even thought I might like a career as a musician or singer. But my father longed for me to audition for the Jim McKee Singers. It was made up of college-age students who traveled in the summer. My father was a powerful Christian, and his greatest joy was for me to sing with them during one of their summer tours."

Callie closed her eyes, wondering how far she could get before she lost control. David shifted his fingers to her arm, caressing her the way a father calms his child.

"I arranged for a tryout and waited in an office set up near the college for the local auditions. I felt more and more nervous as each person went in and left. Soon, I was alone. He came to the door and called me in."

"Who, Callie? Who was he?"

She swallowed, struggling to speak his name. "The director...J-Jim McKee." Her lips stammered the name.

"So what happened?"

She felt David tense, almost as if he could guess what she was going to say, but his eyes only emanated tenderness.

She returned to the story beginning with the *click* of the lock. "'You're nervous enough, I'm sure,' he said to me as he bolted the door. 'We don't want anyone popping in and making things worse, do we?'"

As if marching through her dream, she led David through the audition. "Then Jim McKee led me to the couch, and kept calling me his 'little meadow-lark.' My poor mother called me that a few months ago, and I panicked. I can't hear that word without remembering."

David leaned over to kiss her cheek. "It's okay, Callie. I love you."

"How can you love me, David? You already know what happened." The sobs broke from her throat, and she buried her face in her hands. "I was a virgin. And he took the most precious gift I longed to share with a husband someday. He raped me, David."

Chapter Seventeen

David drew her into his arms, holding her as she wept and rocked her as he would a child. "It wasn't your fault, Callie. You didn't make it happen. It wasn't your fault."

Seven years of pain and sorrow flooded from her in a torrent of hot tears. His murmured words lulled her. When she gathered her strength, she lifted her head, fearing to look in his eyes, but there, she saw only his gentle understanding.

"I've kept that a secret so long, David."

"Why? That's what I don't understand. Why? How many other young women's lives did that demon destroy?"

"I didn't have the courage to tell my parents. My father idolized the man. He wouldn't have accepted that Jim McKee would do something like that." She searched his face for his understanding. "I thought my dad would blame me, think I had been so awed that I was a willing partner. I don't know. I thought

I could wash it away with soap and water and prayers.''

"Callie, my love, you suffered too long.''

"I read in the paper a few years ago that he died suddenly from a heart attack. *David, I was happy.* I'm ashamed of myself, but I was happy he died.''

David buried his face in her hair. She didn't know what he felt. But his eyes had said he understood, and that's what mattered.

She filled her lungs with healing air and released a ragged sigh. "You know, deep inside I've felt so much guilt. I've wondered if I *did* do something to make him think I wanted him.'' She sighed. "Do you know what sticks in my mind?''

He shook his head.

"I remember my deep breath and the buttons gaping on my blouse. I kept asking myself, did I tempt him? Did he think I did it on purpose, that it was a come-on?''

David closed his eyes and shuddered. "Callie, how many women in the world take deep breaths and their buttons pull on their blouses? Do you think it's their announcement to the world that they want to be raped? I can't believe you've worried all these years about that.''

"I was barely a woman then, naive and so innocent...until that terrible day.''

Helplessness washed over her again as she recalled the day she realized she was pregnant. How could she tell her parents then about the horrible event she'd kept from them? That was the moment she decided to let them think the baby growing inside her was fathered by a college student. Why destroy everything they believed? She let them accept her lie.

And now, how could she tell David? He and Sara had chanced everything, even Sara's life, to have a child, and Callie walked away from hers. Maybe the rape wasn't her fault. But losing her child was.

An abortion had been out of the question. God would never forgive her for taking the life of an innocent child. Despite her supposed wisdom, she'd never forgive herself for agreeing to the adoption. How could she tell David?

The silence lingered, and David held her close in his arms.

"David?" she murmured.

"Yes." He pulled his face from her hair and looked into her eyes, questioning.

"Do you understand why I'm afraid? I don't know if I can ever love a man fully without those memories filling my mind. Even your innocent touch scares me sometimes."

"I sensed your fear, Callie, and I didn't understand. I thought it was *me*."

"Oh, no, it isn't you."

"I know that now. And now that I understand, we can work on it, Callie. We'll take it slow. One step at a time. You can learn that being loved is a gentle, powerful experience. *Love,* Callie—love is a gift from God. A wonderful, pure gift."

Tears rose in David's eyes, and for the first time, Callie saw them spill down his cheeks. Her stomach knotted when she saw his sorrow—sorrow he had hidden for so long.

"You're crying." Callie reached up to wipe away

the tears from his cheeks. She kissed his moist eyes and buried her face in his neck.

David's heart reeled at her tenderness. She was not alone in bearing shame for so many years. "I'm crying for both of us. We've both carried secrets longer than we should."

"Secrets? You mean Sara's pregnancy and—"

"Yes, I went against God's wishes and demanded an abortion. I didn't want her to die, and I knew if she carried the baby, she couldn't have the treatment she needed. But Sara refused, and we waited too long. God punished me for my selfishness."

Callie looked at him, her face filled with confusion. "She was too far in her pregnancy for an abortion?"

He didn't comment, leaving her to accept his silence as his answer. Sara had wanted a baby so badly. He remembered the anger he had felt shortly before she died, how he blamed her pregnancy for her short life. Shaking his fist at God for their losses.

David pulled himself from his sad musings. "Callie, we both have some issues to deal with, but doing it together will give us strength. Love is a mighty healer."

He saw in her face understanding and acceptance. He lowered his lips to hers, and this time, she didn't recoil, but raised her mouth to meet his. Gently their lips joined, and she offered him the love that had lain buried inside her.

When they parted, he held her close, praying that the healing for both of them had already begun.

Callie leaped from bed the next morning. The clock read ten. She'd not slept that late in years. What about

Nattie? She threw on her robe and darted across the hall. Nattie was not there. Her bed was unmade, her pajamas in a pile on the floor.

Callie hurried back to her room, completed the most rudimentary cleansing ritual and threw on a pair of slacks and a top. As she dashed down the staircase, she saw David and Nattie at breakfast. Embarrassed at her lateness, she slowed her pace and worked at regaining her composure.

At the bottom of the stairs, a bouquet of fresh flowers sat on the foyer table. At its base lay a card with her name scrawled on the envelope. David caught her eye as she stood in the foyer, and she nodded, touched that he had sent her flowers already, so early in the morning.

But the biggest surprise occurred when she opened the card. The flowers were from John. She flushed, knowing she had to call him immediately after breakfast, to thank him and give him some kind of explanation as to why she couldn't go out with him again.

She hurried into the dining room.

"Callie." Nattie giggled. "You didn't wake me up. Daddy said you overslept."

"Good morning." David eyed her with a searching look. "I believe you overslept."

"I did, didn't I. And why aren't you at work?"

He grinned. "Guilty as charged. And the flowers?"

"You got flowers," Nattie chimed.

Callie nodded. "From John." She wrinkled her nose. "I guess I owe him a telephone call."

"I guess," David said with a hint of jealousy. "What would make him send you a bouquet, I wonder?"

"Guilt? Payola?"

"Blackmail?" His grin grew. "Whatever. Call him, please."

"I will. I promise. By the way, I agreed to fill in as the pianist. Pam Ingram is leaving. She's expecting a baby and doesn't have time to handle the piano and choir right now."

"Pianist and choir director?"

"No. You heard me. *Pianist.* You're the choir director."

"Was."

"We'll see."

"I repeat, *was.*"

She gave him a grin, not saying another word. They enjoyed breakfast together, then David hurried off to work. Later in the afternoon, Agnes called Callie to the front door. She descended the stairs with Nattie on her heels and halted in surprise halfway down.

"More flowers?" she asked, gaping at a delivery man holding a huge package wrapped in floral paper.

"Must be a special occasion," he said. "This is the second bouquet I've delivered here."

She swallowed. "Not really. Just a coincidence." She took the bouquet from him and closed the screen door.

Nattie skipped around her in excitement. "More flowers?"

"Looks like it, doesn't it?"

Callie pulled the protective paper from the magnificent arrangement of mixed flowers: lilies, orchids, roses. John's simple vase looked sad by comparison. She didn't need to open the card to know the source. A grin crept to her lips.

"Who are they from, Callie?"

"Your daddy, I think." Callie pulled the card from the envelope. *I love you. Never forget. David.* She laughed, seeing the sense of competition John's bouquet had aroused. Then her stomach churned as she recalled her promise: she needed to march to the telephone without delay and talk to John.

Callie thanked John by telephone for the flowers and made arrangements to practice on the church piano. Though two pianos were available at the house, her "practice" was an excuse to see him. She reviewed a variety of ways she might tell him about David and her, but nothing felt comfortable.

A cooling air washed over her as she entered the church. The stained-glass windows held the sun's scorching rays at bay. She headed down the aisle, and by the time she reached the piano, John was coming through a side door. But to her dismay, Mary Beth followed behind him.

His sister wore a bright smile painted on her lips, and the look gave Callie an eerie feeling. In a flash, she knew what Mary Beth was thinking. If Callie was dating John, David was "available." She had bad news for both of them.

John stepped to her side. "I appreciate your willingness to fill in here. I'm looking for a regular pianist, I promise, but it may take some time. We don't have too many accomplished musicians hanging around Bedford."

"As long as you know this is temporary," she reminded him.

Mary Beth fanned her face with her hand. "Whew,

you saved me, Callie. I play a little, and John was trying to coerce me.''

Callie bit her tongue. If she had had any idea Mary Beth played, she wouldn't have volunteered—but it was too late now. "Well, I'm glad to hear you can play, Mary Beth. I do plan to visit my mom in Indianapolis. I haven't seen her in a while, and I'm feeling guilty.''

Mary Beth raised her hand to her throat with a titter. "Oh, my, I guess I shouldn't have spoken.''

She leaned intimately toward Callie. "And how are things with you? I understand you had a nice evening. And flowers. He sent you flowers." Her voice lilted with feigned enthusiasm.

"Yes, we had a nice time, but I didn't expect flowers.''

Mary Beth took a step backward. "I suppose I should leave and let the two of you talk privately.''

She needed to act now or never. "No, Mary Beth, don't go. I have something to tell both of you.''

John's face brightened, then faded when he looked at her expression. Mary Beth had a similar reaction.

Callie cleared her throat. "I don't want to mislead you. I had a lovely time. The food was excellent, and I enjoyed the concert. But I'm afraid I can't accept any more invitations.''

"You can't?" John asked.

Mary Beth's head pivoted from one to the other.

"That evening, David and I came to…an understanding.''

Mary Beth gasped. "An understanding?''

"Yes, we realize that we've grown to…care very deeply for each other, and we—we've fallen in love.''

"Fallen in love." The words escaped them in unison like the chorus of a Greek tragedy.

Callie looked at them. "I hope you can be happy for us."

"Happy?" John looked bemused, then his brows unfurrowed. "Happy, yes. I'm happy for you."

She watched him struggle to maintain a neutral expression. Mary Beth's face registered pure frustration.

"Well, I hope under the circumstances," Mary Beth said, her face pinched, "that you don't plan to continue living together in the same house."

Callie's heart dropped. The thought hadn't occurred to her. But she had to live here. How would she and David know if they could work through their problems? Yet how could she explain the situation to others—once Mary Beth spread the news?

Callie leveled her stare at Mary Beth. "We don't live in the house alone, as you know. Agnes and Nattie are both there. I don't believe in premarital relationships, Mary Beth, if that's what you're insinuating." She almost became catty, wanting to add the words, *"Perhaps you do."* But God intervened and removed the words from her lips.

"I'm not insinuating anything. I just wouldn't want others to think differently."

John pressed his sister's arm. "I don't see how others will think anything, Mary Beth. No one knows this, except you and me. And we won't spread idle gossip, will we?"

Mary Beth grasped the neck of her blouse for a second time. "Why...no. I certainly wouldn't spread gossip."

"Then I don't believe we have a problem at all."

Callie wanted to hug him, but instead, she extended her hand. "Thank you, John, for understanding."

Mary Beth hovered as if waiting to receive her thank you, but Callie sat at the piano to practice.

Chapter Eighteen

No matter what John had said to make things better, Callie couldn't forget his sister's words. Was it wrong for her to stay at the house now that she and David had admitted their love for each other? Wonderful, fulfilled days passed by, and though they said nothing to Nattie, the child seemed to understand changes had occurred. And her joy had grown as much as theirs.

September was nearly on their doorstep, and Nattie would soon begin school. With her debut into the world of education, Callie faced a decision. What reason did she have to stay in Bedford? The time had come to talk honestly with David.

But Callie's procrastination had blossomed into avoidance. Today she set a deadline. One week. Within the week, she had to broach the subject of leaving. She couldn't stay in the house under the circumstances, no matter what her heart said.

Callie descended the staircase to a flutter of activity. Yesterday David had announced he'd invited their old housekeeper, Miriam, to dinner. With improved health, she had come to Bedford to visit her sister.

At the bottom of the stairs, Nattie clung to the banister, staring at the door and awaiting Miriam's arrival. At the sound of an automobile, Nattie raced to the door and tugged it open.

As soon as Callie saw her, she understood why Miriam held a special place in their hearts. Stepping from the car was a woman who fulfilled everyone's dream of a roundish, warm, lovable fairy godmother. Her face glimmered with animation and love as she threw her ample arms around Nattie and David.

Callie waited inside, allowing their welcome to be unburdened by introductions. David helped Miriam through the door, and Callie met her in the foyer.

The elderly woman moved cautiously forward, a cane in her left hand, and Callie joined her in welcome. "I'm so happy to meet you. I've heard nothing but wonderful things about you."

Miriam's eyes twinkled. "And I've heard nothing but wonderful things about you." She wrapped one arm around Callie's shoulders, giving her a warm hug.

"Come into the parlor, Miriam. We'll sit until dinner's ready." There, David guided her to a comfortable chair. Nattie clung to her side and leaned against the chair arm, as Miriam settled herself.

"I'd hold you on my lap, precious, but I'm not sure my old legs will bear the weight. You've grown so big since I last saw you. It seems years, rather than months."

Nattie stood straight as if pulled by a string. "I forgot. Agnes said I could help set the table." She skipped from the room, as the others chuckled at her enthusiasm.

"David, what a joy to see her so well." Miriam turned toward Callie. "I know we have this young lady to thank."

Callie murmured a thank you, as Miriam continued. "When I left, my heart was nearly broken, seeing Nattie so distraught. David had already gone through enough without that burden."

"I've enjoyed every moment I've spent with Nattie," Callie said. "I've had the rare pleasure of watching her blossom. It's like a special gift from God."

"I'm sure it is," she said. "And now, David, what's happening with you?"

"Seeing Nattie get better has been amazing. And I might add, meeting Callie has been a blessing for me, too."

A healthy grin curved Miriam's mouth, and her eyes twinkled. "Am I to understand you two have— how should I put it—an understanding?"

Callie glanced at David with a shy grin.

He nodded. "Yes, you could call it that. Callie has brought me back to life as much as she has Nat."

Miriam turned to Callie. "Then, I thank you. You've made an old woman feel very happy."

Callie laughed. "Thanks. We're a pretty happy bunch."

"And we'll be even happier when we eat. Let me check on dinner." David jumped up and left the room.

Miriam checked the doorway, then faced Callie. "While he's gone, I want to thank you privately. I love this family like my own, and my heart was heavy with all the sadness in this house. But today, I feel love—and best of all, promise.''

"Thank you. When I first came, I thought David was a grouchy, unloving, hard-nosed man. At times he was, but I soon found the real David underneath all that cover-up.''

"David hardened himself. He blamed himself for Sara's death, I know. Letting her get pregnant, and then losing the baby. But when they got Nattie, what joy! She was the answer to their prayers.''

"Losing the baby? You mean Sara had a miscarriage. I didn't know that.'' Callie's stomach knotted. David's words echoed in her mind, *"God punished me for my selfishness."* Is that what he'd meant?

"Oh, yes, such sadness that day.''

"I can imagine their joy when Nattie arrived.''

"Yes, but short-lived.'' Miriam's old grief resurfaced in her voice.

"Only four years, I understand.''

Miriam lowered her eyes and a look of disapproval swept over her. "Yes, Sara was a lovely woman... David knew she had cancer when they married.''

Callie nodded. "Yes, he told me.'' Obviously, Miriam had stronger feelings than she allowed herself to say.

The older woman regrouped. "But the four years with Nattie were wonderful years for them both. Right up to the end.''

David's footsteps signaled his return. He came through the doorway with his hands outstretched. "Dinnertime. Have you ever heard sweeter words?''

Callie helped Miriam from the chair and whispered

in her ear, "I always thought the sweetest words were 'I love you'—but you know men."

The two women chuckled, and David raised an eyebrow at them.

They lingered over a dinner of good food, reminiscences and laughter—until the telephone rang.

Agnes summoned Callie.

It was Ken. "It's Mom," he said. "She had another stroke. More serious this time."

"Oh, no, Ken. I've been meaning to visit, but I haven't. I feel so terrible. I'll leave right away."

"You can wait if you'd rather. I'll keep you posted. No sense in rushing here tonight."

Callie clenched the receiver. "No, I want to come now. I'll feel better. I won't sleep a wink if I stay here."

"Okay. Give me a call when you arrive. If I'm not home, I'll be here at the hospital."

"It'll take me three hours or so, Ken. It'll be late. Nine-thirty or ten, maybe. So don't worry."

"Callie, drive carefully."

She placed the receiver in the cradle and turned toward the dining room. She hated to put a damper on the visit.

As she entered the room, David rose. "Is something wrong?"

When the words stumbled from her tongue, she fought back her tears. "My mom's had a bad stroke. I have to go home tonight."

"Get ready, Callie, and I'll drive you," David said. "I don't want you to go alone."

"No, I need my car while I'm there. I'm fine,

please. You go ahead and enjoy your visit. I'll run up and pack. As soon as I know something, I'll call.''

When Callie arrived, she went directly to the hospital. Grace lay sleeping, connected to a machine that hummed and flashed numbers measuring her vital signs. Ken stepped from the bedside and wrapped his arm around Callie.

"She's about the same. She seems to be out of danger, but you can see the stroke has affected her this time.''

Callie leaned over the bed and saw her mother's mouth twisted to one side. "So how much damage? Can they tell yet?''

"No. They'll run some tests in the morning. The doctor said her speech will be affected, at least for a while.'' He motioned to the chair. "Sit here for a few minutes. I'll take a walk and stretch my legs.''

Callie nodded and eased herself into the chair. Pushing her arm through the bed's protective bars, she patted her mother's hand. Tears rose in her eyes, and she felt angry at herself for not having taken the time to come up for a visit.

She rested her head against the high chair back, and her mind filled with prayers. As her thoughts turned to God, she remembered her quandary— whether to stay in Bedford or come home. Maybe this was God's way of intervening. Perhaps her decision would be made for her.

Ken returned, bringing her a cup of coffee. They stayed by their mother's side until their eyelids drooped, then agreed that sitting there all night was foolish. Grace was out of danger, and they needed their rest.

Walking into the night air, Callie looked up into the sky, wondering if indeed God was directing her. If her mother needed her here, she would move back to Indianapolis. She had little choice.

In the morning, Callie called the nurse's station. Grace had rested during the night, and remained the same. Before leaving for the hospital, Callie called David and promised to phone later when she knew more.

By the time she reached the hospital, Ken had not arrived, and Callie stood alone in the doorway of Grace's room. Her mother's eyes were closed, but as Callie neared the bed, Grace opened them with a look of confusion.

"Everything's fine, Mom. You're in the hospital."

Grace opened her mouth, but the muddled words filled her eyes with fear.

"Don't try to talk, Mom. Just rest. The doctor will be in soon, and we'll know more then." Callie adjusted the chair and sat beside her. "If you need me, I'm right here."

She took her mother's hand and gave it a squeeze. And to her relief, Grace exerted a faint answering pressure. Callie clasped her mother's hand, thanking God.

Grace drifted into a fitful sleep, and Callie waited, speaking with nurses as they came in and out to check machines and the IVs, but they said little about her mother's condition.

Ken arrived, and two doctors followed on his heels,

then conferred outside the room. Callie rose and met them in the hallway, while Ken stood beside Grace. When they entered, Ken kissed his mother's cheek and joined Callie.

"They suggested we go down for coffee while they examine her. He'll catch us later. Okay?" Callie asked.

Ken agreed, and they hurried to the cafeteria and moved quickly along the food line. Balancing her tray, Callie found a table near an outside window. They ate in silence, until Callie could gather her thoughts.

"I'm trying to decide what to do, Ken. Nattic has improved so much. She'll be starting school in a couple more weeks, and I suppose I should come back home and stay with Mom."

"I thought the last time I talked to you things were going well with you and David. Didn't you say a little romance was cooking?" Ken lifted his coffee cup and drank.

"That's another issue. I'm not sure if I should stay at the house under the circumstances. What will people say?" She leaned back against her chair, her fork poised in her hand. "But if I'm not there, we have little hope for a relationship, either. A two-hour drive each way doesn't encourage a budding romance."

"It's your call, sis."

"I know. But I'm so confused." She placed the fork on her plate and rubbed her temples.

"Well, don't try to make decisions now. Let's see what the doctors say. Mom may be in better shape than we think."

"I don't know if that really solves my dilemma. I

still think I should come home." Her hands knotted on the table.

He placed his hand on hers. "Don't ruin your life, Callie. You overthink things sometimes. Try to be patient. Let's take one problem at a time. We're worried about Mom right now."

When they finished eating, they returned to Grace's room and met the doctor outside her door.

"So what do you think, Dr. Sanders?" Callie asked. "Any idea yet what happened?"

"Let me use layman's terms."

"Thanks. But I might mention I'm a nurse."

"Good. That could be helpful. Your mother apparently had an embolism. A blood clot broke loose from somewhere in her body, perhaps the heart. It often travels through the arterial stream into the cerebral cortex. When the clot lodges somewhere along its path, it can stop the flow of blood to the brain. In your mother's case, it did, and the stroke resulted."

Ken's face tensed. "So what happens now? Do you know how bad it is?"

"We'll run more tests, but we know she has some paralysis. She'll need physical therapy, and we'll begin that as soon as she's strong enough. Speech therapy will begin as soon as she's alert. Sometimes we have to wait two or three months before we see if she'll have permanent damage."

Ken's eyes widened. "Two or three months? You mean, we just have to sit and wait?"

"We'll do what we can." He looked at Callie. "And you might be able to speed up the process if you're willing to handle additional physical therapy at home."

Helping with Mom's treatment meant staying in Indianapolis. Nattie's face rose in Callie's mind, and a lonely feeling engulfed her.

"Good. Right now, your mother has IVs, but later she'll be on a variety of medications. An anticoagulant to keep her blood from clotting, and a vasodilator to keep the arteries open. If she has a narrowing or blockage in the carotid artery, she'll need surgery. Right now, your guess is as good as mine. The test will answer a lot of questions."

Ken glanced at Callie.

She shrugged. "We'll wait, then, until you have more information."

The doctor nodded. "You're welcome to visit for a while, but I suggest you let your mother rest as much as possible. Later today, we'll run the tests. Why not stay for a few more minutes, and then go on home? Come back this evening, if you like, and by tomorrow we should have some answers."

Ken nodded. "How about it, Callie?"

She heaved a sigh. "Not much we can do now, I suppose." She looked at the physician. "And we should follow doctor's orders."

With a gentle grin, the doctor rested his hand on her arm. "I only hope your mother's as good at following orders as you are."

According to the test reports, Grace's prognosis gave Callie hope. The week passed during which she was scheduled for daily therapy. Another week or so in the hospital, Dr. Sanders said, and her mother could go home.

The news still lay unsettled in Callie's mind. She

sat in her mother's house, staring at the telephone. She had promised to call David, but she had delayed for a full week, wanting to clarify her decision.

David had sent flowers to Grace at the hospital, and another lovely bouquet sat on a nearby table. The brilliant colors should have brightened Callie's evening, but they didn't. Her thoughts were too muddled. She missed David and Nattie. But when Grace was released, she'd need help. Callie knew she had to provide it.

She raised the receiver and punched in the numbers. David's voice echoed across the line.

"How are you two?" she asked.

"We miss you. How are things there?"

"Better. Mom started therapy, and I'm happy to say, she's doing pretty well. Her speech is slurred, but I can understand her. And she forgets words once in a while."

David chuckled. "I do that without a stroke. How about movement?"

"She can't walk by herself yet. But things are promising. It'll take time. She'll have to continue therapy when she gets home."

He sighed. "So that means...?"

"So that means, I'll be coming to Bedford for my things."

Silence.

David finally spoke. "Then you'll go back for a while. I understand. Your mother needs you."

Callie closed her eyes to catch the tears that formed. "Not for a while, David. I'm coming back for good."

Chapter Nineteen

David hovered in her doorway, the blood in his veins as frozen as if he were an ice sculpture. Callie stood at the closet, packing. His wonderful new life was melting away; where his hopes and dreams had been, he saw only empty space.

"Callie, can't you listen to reason?"

"You mean *your reason,* David, not mine."

He strode across the room to her side. "I know your mother needs you now, but not forever. Please, we can't manage here without you, and I don't mean taking care of Nattie. We both love you. You're part of our lives."

She swung to face him. "Please, don't make this harder than it is. I love you, too, David, but we're both dealing with issues from the past. I'm not sure this relationship can go anywhere. Especially now, since someone made me think." Her eyes closed for a heartbeat. "I can't ruin your reputation or mine."

"What are you talking about? 'Ruin your reputation or mine'? That doesn't make sense."

"Yes, it does. Nat's fine now. She doesn't need me. So what purpose do I have living here? I'm a paid...what? You tell me." She grasped his arms. "I'm a pretty expensive baby-sitter, wouldn't you say?"

Tears spilled from her eyes and ran down her cheeks.

"Oh, Callie, what do you think you are—a kept woman?" David slid his arms around her back. "God knows that we need you here. I don't care what others might say. And why would they? Who would say anything?"

Callie shook her head without answering.

"Everyone knows about Nattie's problems. For you to walk in and out of our lives when you mean so much to her is unthinkable. She lost her mother, and now you—someone she's grown to love. Who would put such crazy thoughts in your head?"

David's mind swam. *Pastor John? Agnes?* None of it made sense. "You're a Christian. You serve the church. No one would think wrong of you for being here. And what about Nattie?"

"But she's well, David. She doesn't *need* me anymore."

He dropped his arms to his sides and spun away. "No? You think she doesn't need you. Do you know where she is right now?" He whirled around to face her. "She's crying in her room. Nattie loves you. When you came, I didn't think about her loving you. All I thought was that I needed someone to make her better. I never thought I would hurt her."

Callie covered her face with her hands, and remorse spilled over him for the sorrow he had created by his words. "I'm not trying to make you feel guilty. I'm only trying to help you understand how much we love you."

"I'm sorry, David. I've given this a lot of thought. I pray I'm doing the right thing. If I'm wrong, I hope God will help me make it right. That's all I can say. I spent my life bearing a secret anger toward my parents. My mom is the only parent I have left to whom I can make retribution for my feelings. I have to do this."

David closed his eyes and filled his lungs with air. Why did she feel anger toward her parents? He didn't understand her cryptic comment. "I know you want to be with your mother, Callie. And Indianapolis is only two hours away. We'll work things out. Remember our 'deal' a while ago? We agreed to pray for each other. Like Jesus said, 'Where two or three are gathered in my name, I am with them.' We'll leave it in God's hands."

He moved to her side again and held her close. Her heart pounded against his chest, answering his own thudding rhythm. "I love you, Callie." He tilted her face to his. "I have faith in us." His lips touched hers lightly, then he backed away and left, knowing his life would soon be as lonely as the room she was vacating.

Callie struggled to see the road through her tears on her return to Indianapolis. Signing adoption papers had been the hardest thing she'd ever done. Saying goodbye to Nattie was the second. And saying goodbye to David... Callie had no words for the way she felt. She loved them both, but too many things stood in their way. Mary Beth's words hammered in her mind. David still struggled with Sara's death, and Callie had yet to heal from the rape and the adoption. Like someone who carries baskets of bricks up a hill, she carried the weight of Jim McKee's sin on her shoulders.

So often when she looked at Nattie, she imagined her own child. Did her daughter have a halo of blond curls? Was she loved? Was she learning about Jesus? Callie couldn't bear to think the worst. She longed to know—her heart ached. And all the love she had denied herself for years had risen like a wonderful gift and showered down on Nattie. And again Callie was letting a child go. Callie longed for a release. Would telling David about her own child help to heal the wounds? Now she would never know.

Since the telephone call, her thoughts had been filled with worry about her mother. But as she left Bedford, her talk with Miriam drifted into her mind. David hadn't told her Sara had miscarried. Yet he'd told her about wanting the abortion. Callie's head spun with disjointed bits of information, spilled out like pieces of one of Nattie's puzzles. Why didn't David feel God's forgiveness when Nattie was born? Why did he cling to his anger? God had given him a second chance—Nattie.

Finally, she turned her concerns to her present problem—Grace. Would Mom listen to her—as her nurse, and not as her daughter? What might that do to their relationship, which she had hoped to heal? Her head ached with wondering.

The next days flew past with preparations for Grace's return: a hospital bed, therapy training, treatment scheduling, grocery shopping. Yet keeping busy didn't help Callie feel less sad or lonely.

David persisted. He phoned, sent flowers and wrote notes on Missing You cards, but Callie clung to her decision. She believed God's hand had guided her.

Grace's day of homecoming arrived, and Callie stood beside her hospital bed packing her belongings. "Anxious to get home, Mom?"

Grace nodded as she had begun to do, avoiding her distorted voice.

"Talk, Mom. No head-nods. The more you talk, the quicker you'll have your old voice back."

Grace clamped her lips together like a disobedient child.

"Very adult of you, Mom." Callie shook her head in frustration. She had watched hospital films and talked to the psychologist for tips on helping Grace and being supportive. She already felt like a failure.

As she finished packing, Dr. Sanders appeared at the doorway. "So today's the big day? How are you feeling?"

Grace shrugged, then struggled to get out a thick-sounding "Fine."

"Good. I have your prescriptions written out for you. And you're a lucky woman to have a daughter who's a nurse."

"I'm not sure that will go over too well," Callie said. "She's going to resent me."

Dr. Sanders patted Callie's hand. "She'll be fine." He turned to Grace. "Now, you'll listen to your daughter, right? She's trained to help you, and you'll have to mind her. If not, you'll end up back here. I know you don't want that.''

Grace's eyes widened, but she kept her lips pressed together.

Dr. Sanders pointed to her mouth. ''And you have to speak, Grace. You'll never talk if you don't practice.''

He turned to Callie. ''We'll send the speech therapist out three times a week, and then count on you to do the rest.''

''That's fine. I've had instructions, and I can handle the therapy—if she'll listen.'' She directed her last words to Grace.

He spoke for a moment with Grace, and when he left, Callie gathered up the overnight bag and parcels and headed to her car.

Grace was wheeled outside and eased into the car. The trip home was silent, except for Callie's own running monologue. And she breathed a relieved sigh when Ken's car pulled into the driveway behind them.

''Glad you're here,'' she said, sliding from the car. She closed her door. ''I didn't know if I could get Mom in alone. Besides, I need a little moral support.''

''You look beat already,'' Ken said, standing at the trunk, as they unloaded the wheelchair.

She looked at him, shaking her head. ''I'm afraid this'll be the undoing of Mother and me. I hoped, coming home, we could smooth out our differences, but she's being terribly belligerent. Like a child.''

Ken rolled his eyes. ''We'll just have to be patient. She'll come around.''

She rested her hand on his shoulder. ''And don't forget, I'll need a break once in a while. I can't do this alone or I'll end up in a hospital...and it won't be *medical* hospital."

Ken slammed the trunk. "No one would ever notice."

"Thanks." She poked his arm.

He rolled the wheelchair to the car door, and with his strong arms settled Grace into the seat. Together, they hoisted Grace up the porch stairs into the house and into the hospital bed, as the patient grunted and pointed.

Hands on her hips, Callie stood beside them "Make her talk, Ken." She scowled at her mother. "We'll have no grunting or pointing in this house."

Grace glowered back as much as her face would allow, and Callie covered a snicker. Her heart broke for her mother, but she knew she'd better learn to laugh if they were to survive.

When Grace was settled, Callie invited Ken into the kitchen for a sandwich. He stretched his legs in front of him, twiddling his thumbs, as Callie buttered the bread. "Do you think you can do this?" he asked.

"Oh, they say God never gives us more than we can handle." She turned to face him. "But I think He's pushing it this time."

Ken threw his head back and laughed. "I was thinking the same thing. Hang in there, and I'll do what I can to help."

"Great, but I won't hold my breath."

David sent two more bouquets the following week—one for her, and the other for Grace. Callie missed him more than she could say. The situation hadn't eased. Grace fought her at every turn, and her nerves pulsed like wired dynamite.

One day, Callie was sitting in the kitchen, nibbling a sandwich that she could barely swallow, when the telephone rang. When she heard David's voice, her hand shook. She longed to tell him how awful things were, but instead she inquired about him, avoiding what was in her heart.

Finally she asked, "How's Nat?"

"Lonesome." A heavy silence hung on the line. "So am I, Callie. Nothing seems worth much anymore."

She refused to respond. She'd say far more than was safe to admit. "How's Nat's school? Is she doing okay?"

She waited. A chill ruffled through her. "Is something wrong, David?"

"I don't want to burden you. You have enough problems."

She stiffened. "Don't leave me hanging, David. What's wrong." Her voice sounded strained to her ears. "I'm sorry, David, but you've upset me. Is something wrong with Nattie?"

"She's...beginning to withdraw again. Not like before, but she's not herself. I know she misses you. It'll pass with time. Her teacher was concerned, but I explained that...well, I didn't want to get into a lengthy discussion. I said her mother had died recently. I figured that would explain it."

If she'd felt stress before, she felt a thousand times worse hearing his words. "I don't know what to say. Even if I wanted to come back, I can't. Mom needs too much right now, and Ken works full time. He gives me a break once in a while, but I'm it, David. I'm the caregiver here."

He sighed. "I know. I know. I'm trying to think of something."

When she hung up, she covered her face and wept. She felt pity for everyone: Grace, David, Nattie and herself. When her tears ended, she splashed water on her eyes and planted a smile on her lips. Her wristwatch signaled Grace's therapy—and if Callie didn't smile, she'd scream.

"Look at you, Mom," Ken said, as Grace shuffled her feet across the floor while leaning heavily on her walker.

A twisted grin covered Grace's face; she looked as pleased as a toddler learning to take her first steps.

Callie stood nearby, watchful for any problems, but Grace moved steadily along. "Mom's worked hard," she said to Ken. "It makes it worthwhile, doesn't it, Mom? At least, you can get up and move around a little."

Grace grunted a "yes." Her speech had improved, too, turning their hope to reality.

Callie kept her eyes focused on Grace. "See if you can make it to the living room, Mom. You can sit in there for a change."

Grace heaved her shoulders upward as she moved the walker. When she was seated, Callie made a pot of tea and brought out some freshly baked cookies for a celebration. As difficult as it had been, she could see that Grace was mending.

As they talked, the telephone rang, and Callie left

the living room to answer it in the kitchen. Something inside her told her the caller was David.

"Don't say a word, Callie, but Nattie and I are coming to Indianapolis to see you."

"Please, David, no. I'm still miserable. I don't think I could bear to see you...and not Nattie. I'll cry for sure."

"Good. Tears soften the heart, Callie, my love. You might as well give up. I'm coming. Nattie will be terribly disappointed if I tell her you don't want us to come."

"Oh, David. Don't say that. Come, then. I'll be here...forever."

"Maybe not. I think I have a solution."

Chapter Twenty

Callie's heart did cartwheels when she saw Nattie through the window. The child darted up the porch before David could catch her. Callie flung open the door and knelt to embrace her; Nattie flew into her arms and buried her face in Callie's neck.

Her small, muffled voice sounded on Callie's cheek. "I miss you."

"I miss you, too, Nat. Terribly." Callie raised her eyes toward David. "I miss all of you."

"Aren't you coming home?" Nattie asked.

The word *home* tore through her. Bedford was more home to her than her mother's house. The answer caught in her throat. She swallowed, and avoided a direct answer. "My mom is sick right now, Nat, and I have to take care of her."

Nattie tilted her head back and searched Callie's face. "Is she going to die?"

"No, she's getting better. But you know what? She

won't talk much at all. Do you remember someone who didn't want to talk much a while ago?''

Nattie hung her head shyly and nodded. But her head popped up with her next words. "Is your mommy sad?''

Callie grinned. "No, not sad.'' She glanced up at David. "More like 'mad.' As mad as a wet hen, in fact.''

Nattie giggled at the old saying.

"Well, let's not stand in the doorway. Come in.'' Callie rose, took Nattie by the hand, and moved so David could enter.

He stepped inside and slipped his arm cautiously around her waist, as Nattie eyed them. "How are you?''

Callie lowered her eyes. "Miserable. And you?''

"Terribly miserable.''

Nattie pushed her shoulders forward, squeezing her hands between her knees, and chuckled. "I'm miserable, too.''

Her words made them smile. Callie gave her another hug. "Well, that's good, then. We're all miserable together.'' She gestured them into the living room. "Have you eaten? Anyone starving?''

"No, we had some breakfast on the way.''

"We stopped at Burger Boy,'' Nattie added.

"Burger Boy, huh?'' Callie gave David a disapproving look.

He wiggled his eyebrows. "They have biscuit breakfasts.''

"Ah. Well, then, how about something to drink and maybe a cookie or two?''

They agreed, and while they waited in the living

room, Callie gathered the drinks and cookies, taking deep breaths to control her wavering emotions. She loved them both, and seeing them today, though wonderful, felt painful, as well.

"Here we go," she said, carrying a tray into the living room and putting the cookies closest to Nattie.

Sinking into a chair, Callie studied David's face. His usual bright, teasing eyes looked shadowed. She gazed at Nattie, longing to speak privately to David. Then an idea struck.

"David, would you and Nat like to say hello to Mom?"

"Sure, if she's up to it."

"Nat, you've never met my mother. I might have a book around here somewhere, and you could show her the pictures and tell her a story. Would you like that? She gets pretty lonely in her room."

Nattie nodded, and Callie hurried to her room. On her bookshelf, she'd kept some favorite children's books. She shuffled through them and located a book of well-known tales and stories illustrated with colorful pictures. Before she returned to the living room, she popped into Grace's room to announce visitors, then left without giving Grace a chance to say no.

In the living room, she handed Nattie the book. "When I was young, this book was one of my favorites."

As soon as Nattie held the book, she flipped through the pages. "I know this story, and this one," she said.

"Good, then let's go in to see my mom."

She took Nattie by the hand, with David following, and headed down the hallway. Grace was staring at the doorway as they entered, looking stressed, probably over Callie's announcement. But when her gaze lit upon Nattie, her face softened. Only the slight tug of paralysis distorted her usual expression.

"Mom, here's David. And Nattie. You've never met her."

David stepped forward, extending his hand. "It's good to see you, Grace. Callie says you're doing great. A little more time, and you'll be back to normal, huh?"

"Oh, I don't know," Grace said, her speech thick and halting.

Nattie stared at Grace and then glanced at Callie. "I thought your mommy didn't talk."

Callie snickered. "Maybe she just doesn't talk to *me*, Nattie." She peered at Grace. Her mother averted her eyes. Instead, she watched Nattie.

"When I was younger, I didn't want to talk," Nattie said, leaning her folded arms on Grace's bed.

"No?" Grace said, not taking her eyes from the child.

"I was too sad."

"Happy now?" Grace laid her hand on Nattie's arms.

"Uh-huh, except Callie went away to take care of you." Nattie glanced at Callie over her shoulder. "I miss her."

Grace's skewed face formed an angled smile. "You do, huh?"

"Yep." Nattie leaned forward and whispered at Grace. "But we came for a visit to tell her to come home."

Grace raised her eyes toward Callie. "Home?" She

reached out and drew her hand over Nattie's blond hair, then nodded. "Yes, I suppose that is her home."

Tears burned behind Callie's eyes, and she quickly changed the topic. "Mom, Nattie wants to show you a picture book. You want to get up in a chair, or would you rather have her up there on the bed with you?"

Grace patted the coverlet beside her, and David boosted the child to the edge of the bed.

"You can get up for lunch, okay? We'll be in the other room for a few minutes. Can you get down by yourself, Nat?"

"I think so." She stared down at the floor.

"If not, give a call, and I'll come running," David said, patting her cheek with his fingers.

Callie and David walked out of the room, leaving Nattie to entertain Grace.

"I think Nat could work wonders with Mother. I haven't seen her so talkative since the stroke. She buttons up when I'm the one she has to talk to."

"But you're the nurse. No one likes nurses. They're too mean, and they make you take medicine and do things you don't want to do."

She returned his tease, rolling her eyes. "Thanks."

"And they always say, 'It's time to take *our* bath.' Have you ever seen a nurse—other than yourself, that is—take a bath?"

She listened to David's chatter, but inside, her stomach dipped on a roller-coaster ride. What would happen now that they were alone? David answered her question. He slid his arm around her waist, drawing her against him. His hand ran up her arm to her face, and he touched her cheek, drawing his fingers along her heating skin to trace her lips.

Her knees wanted to buckle beneath her, and a sensation, beginning as a tingle, grew to an uncontrollable tremor, as his face neared hers. She thought of pulling away, but her desire overpowered her intentions. She met his lips with hers, eagerly savoring the sweetness, and a moan escaped his throat, sending a deepening shudder through her body as her own sigh joined his.

Out of breath, she eased away and gazed into his heavy-lidded eyes. "David, you can't kiss me like this. I can't handle it."

"Good. Let *me* handle things. I refuse to leave this house without knowing you'll come back to us."

"How can I do that? Tell me." She raised her voice overwhelmed by a sense of futility. She longed to be with them in Bedford. No matter what others thought, she loved them and belonged with them.

"Let's sit, and I'll tell you how. I've figured it out. Come." He took her hand and guided her into the living room, and together they sank onto the sofa in each other's arms.

Her first thought was Nattie. What if she saw David's arms around her? "What if Nattie see us?"

"I told her I love you, Callie. And guess what she said."

She could only shake her head.

"She loves you, too. That was her response. And she needs you. She's been so quiet. But as soon as she saw you today, she opened again. Look at her with Grace. She's good for Grace, too."

Callie couldn't deny that. Grace hadn't been so receptive to anyone. Maybe a child's exuberance would bring her out of her self-pitying mode. She thought of her own situation. Nattie had worked a miracle, making her a whole person again.

"So," Callie asked. "What's your plan?"

"Bring your mother to Bedford."

"What?" She scanned his eager face. "I can't do that."

"Why not? Bring her to the house. We have tons of room."

"But it doesn't make sense...does it?"

"It makes all the sense in the world. I've already made arrangements. We'll set the library up as her room. She'll have an easy chair, television, books if she likes to read. There's a telephone there. A bathroom nearby."

"You're overwhelming me." She shook her head in confusion.

"I realized there's no shower on the first floor, except in Agnes's quarters. She said, 'Great, no problem.' So that's solved."

"What about her doctors and medication?"

"Once she's able to get around more, you can bring Grace here for her appointments. And her prescriptions can be filled in Bedford or here. That's not a problem."

Callie stared at him, dazed. "You've thought of everything, I take it."

"Please, don't get upset with me."

"I'm not upset, really. I'm stunned, David. I made a decision that staying in Bedford was the wrong thing to do, and now you're organizing and arranging my life."

"I'm sorry. That was selfish of me to assume that—"

"No, no, I'm not angry. I love you for it, because it means you love me. But I need to think things through."

"I understand, and you'll want to wait until the doctor says it's okay for Grace to travel. But, Callie, we can handle things if we know you're coming home."

"Home?" she said.

"Yes, home." He turned her face to his, and their lips met.

Past fears of intimacy rose inside her, and she tensed for a flickering moment. Then, as quickly, she relaxed her shoulders. With David, she experienced what God meant by loving…giving herself to a special someone and feeling complete.

With his kiss still warm on her lips, Callie rested her head against his shoulder. "David, I can't do anything without Mom's approval. I don't know if she'll be willing to come to Bedford."

"I've prayed." He ran his hand across the back of his neck. "I've prayed, and I believe God heard my prayers. I think Grace will come, Callie. Give her time, but I think she'll come."

She closed her eyes, adding her prayer to David's. Life was nothing without him and Nattie. That's where she belonged. But in all the confusion, she had yet to accomplish what she had set out to do: resolve the hurt that affected her relationship with Grace. She had to forgive and be forgiven.

Forgiving and being forgiven. Such complicated concepts.

She hadn't been totally honest with David, either. Would he forgive her when he learned about her child and the adoption? If only she knew her daughter was happy, maybe she could forgive herself.

But God had given her another child: Nattie. Was this her second chance to make things right?

Chapter Twenty-One

David checked the library for the fifth time. The room looked comfortable. Bed, bedside table, small dresser, all hauled down from an upstairs bedroom. He'd added a television set, and today, a bouquet of fresh flowers had been delivered. He wanted Grace to feel welcome.

The move had been difficult. Callie had been met with resistance from her mother, but finally, Grace had a change of heart. He didn't question the cause, but Callie said it followed on the footsteps of Nattie's second visit to Indianapolis. Nattie had latched onto Grace as she had the first time and had remained at her side. One evening, they sat together in the living room. As David and Callie talked, they grinned, overhearing Grace's and Nattie's conversation from the sofa.

"Tell me about school," Grace said, her speech clearer than it had been on their first visit.

Nattie tilted her head and thought. "Well, the

teacher said I'm a good reader for first grade. And I can print my name and some other words..." She paused and raced across the room to Callie. "Do you have paper and a pencil? I want to show your mommy how I can print."

"Sure, I do," Callie said, and pulled a pad of paper and pencil from a lamp table drawer. "Here, you go."

Nattie returned to Grace, nestled at her side and proceeded to demonstrate her printing talents. David listened to Grace's encouraging comments and then returned to his own conversation.

"Any progress with Grace?" David asked in a near whisper, knowing his plans for them to move to Bedford had not set well.

"She's stubborn, David. I suppose I understand. But I haven't given up."

"She seems to be doing well."

"She is. She's using her own bed now, and she walks with the cane, though one leg still isn't cooperating totally."

"I'd hoped once she got around a little on her own, she might think of Bedford as a vacation," he said.

Callie rolled her eyes. "There's where you made your second mistake. Mom isn't crazy about vacations. She's a homebody."

He glanced at Grace and Nattie, the weight of hopelessness on his chest. His life had been empty and futureless without Callie. Though Nattie had withdrawn after she left, their visit two weeks earlier had seemed to work a miracle. All he could think about was his prayer that Callie would come back to Bedford.

Muddled in his thoughts, Nattie's words pulled him back to the present.

"Could you be my grandma?" she asked, looking into Grace's attentive eyes.

David's heart kicked into second gear. He glanced at Callie and saw that she had heard. He waited for Grace's response, his heartbeat suspended.

She lifted her gnarled hand and patted Nattie's leg, which was snuggled close to her own. "I'd like that, Nattie. You can call me Grandma Grace." Her eyes hadn't shifted from the child's face.

"Could I just call you Grandma?"

Grace's face twisted to a gentle smile. "Whatever makes you happy, child."

"Good," Nattie said, and lifted herself to kiss Grace's cheek.

David's heart melted at the sight, and when he turned to Callie, she was wiping tears from her eyes.

"Sentimental, huh?" she asked.

"Just plain beautiful," David responded.

That day had replayed itself over in his mind for the past two weeks. A week after their last visit, Callie had called to say Grace was becoming more receptive to a trip to Bedford. Today, his dream would become a reality.

Now, glancing out the window once again, David grinned, as he saw Nattie gallop through the autumn leaves gathered in mounds under the elms. She was as anxious as he.

Tired of waiting inside, David tossed on his windbreaker and joined Nattie in the yard. Seeing him, she giggled and filled her arms with leaves, tossing them into the air. As the burnished leaves settled to earth

Callie's car came up the winding driveway. Nattie let out a squeal and ran toward him. Together, they followed the car until it stopped in front of the wide porch.

"Grandma. Callie," Nattie called, racing to the car door.

Callie climbed out and gave Nattie a hug. David opened the passenger door and helped Grace from the car.

He longed to take Callie in his arms, but Grace leaned heavily on him, so he controlled himself. Later, when they were alone, he could welcome her as he longed to do. He eased Grace up the wide steps and across the porch. Agnes greeted them at the door and held it open so Grace had easy access.

"My, now this is what I call a foyer," Grace said, looking wide-eyed around the vast entrance. "Callie didn't quite prepare me for something this elegant."

Nattie jigged around her, encouraging her to follow. "Look, Grandma, here's your bedroom. It's the lib'ary, but now it's your room."

"David didn't want you to climb the stairs," Callie explained. "He has extra bedrooms upstairs. When you're up to it, we can move your things up there, if you'd like."

Grace concentrated on her steps, but shifted her focus for a moment from the floor to Callie's face. "When I can climb those steps, I'll be ready to go back home." She grinned at David. "And you'll probably be ready to kick me out."

Nattie spun around, hearing her words. "We won't kick you out, Grandma. You can stay with me forever."

With a knowing eye, she glanced at Nattie. "Thank you, child. That's the sweetest thing I've ever heard."

Callie leaned close to David's ear. "That's because she doesn't listen to me. Believe it or not, I have said some pretty sweet things."

David winked at her. "I'm sure you have."

Grace raised her head and looked at the two of them. "I may have had a stroke, but I'm not deaf. So quit talking about me."

Nattie grasped her hand. "We have to be nice to Grandma. She's sick."

David and Callie burst into laughter, with Grace's snicker not far behind. Nattie looked at the three of them, then tucked her hands between her knees and joined them with her own giggle.

Callie hung up the telephone and turned to David. "I gather you told Pastor John I was coming back."

He nodded. "Why? Was it supposed to be a secret?"

"No, but he just called to ask me to sing on Sunday. And he told me about the organ, David. I'm really pleased."

"Give thanks to God, not me. He brought me to my senses."

"What do you mean?"

David took her hands in his and kissed them. "My anger was focused in the wrong direction. I've been angry at God for taking Sara and for Nat's problems, instead of being angry at myself. We knew Sara had cancer, but I expected God to work a miracle."

She nodded. "We can't expect miracles."

"No, we can't expect anything, but we need to

have faith. It's the faith that works the miracles. And God hasn't let me down, even when I was being bull-headed. I wanted instant gratification. But sometimes, we have to do a bit of soul-searching before we can appreciate God's will."

"So after some soul-searching, you decided to donate to the organ-repair fund."

"Paid for the repair. I can afford it, and the congregation enjoys the organ music as much as I do."

"It's nice for everyone. I'm glad, David. Oh, and Pastor John mentioned the new organist...with much enthusiasm, I might add." She suspected John valued the organist for more than her musical contributions on Sunday mornings.

"Wait until you see her. She's cute and single. And the right age."

Teasing, Callie arched an eyebrow. "The right age for whom?"

"For Pastor John." He caressed her cheek with the back of his fingers. "*Whom* else?" He gave her a wink.

"Well, I'm glad." She sat next to him on the sofa. "She doesn't happen to have a brother Mary Beth's age, does she?"

"Jealous, are you?" He clasped her hand.

"Should I be?"

"No, but I forgot to tell you what happened while you were gone."

Callie raised both eyebrows this time. "Ah, true confessions?" She curled her legs beneath her and faced him.

"Not quite." His words were accompanied by a chuckle. "But this is about Mary Beth."

Callie's eyes glinted in jest. "And?"

"A day or two after you left, she called, inviting me to dinner."

"And you accepted, I'm sure."

"Anticipating her motive, yes. I wanted to clear up the issue once and for all...and for no other reason."

"I'm certain." Callie batted her eyelashes at him.

David grinned. "Anyway, to get back to the subject—as I intended—"

"Ah, as you intended."

"Yes, as I intended, she let me know she was interested in making my lonely life less lonely."

"Beautifully said."

"Thank you."

Callie draped an arm around his neck. "And what did you say to that?"

"I thanked her graciously, but declined her offer." He filled his lungs. "Actually, I felt terrible for her. She was embarrassed and flustered. She wasn't quite as blunt as I made her out to be, but she did let me know how she felt."

"I hope you were nice when you rejected her."

"As nice as a rejection can be. I said I was in love with you—but that if I weren't, she'd be a likely second." He tilted his head, giving her a coy look.

"Now that's a rejection."

"I didn't really add the last part." He chucked her beneath the chin. "And I told her I planned to do all I could to bring you back to Bedford."

"You did? Really?"

"I did. She handled it quite well, I'd say."

"No weeping or gnashing of teeth?"

"Only a little."

"Good. She can probably handle it better than I can. With weeping, I'm skilled, but gnashing...?" She gave him a silly grin.

After church on Sunday morning, Callie slipped into her casual clothes and went outside. More leaves had fallen overnight, and winter's chill had put a coating of hoarfrost on everything. She drew in a deep breath of frigid air.

In less than a month Thanksgiving would arrive, then Christmas. On Christmas Day her child would be seven, and little more than a month later, Nat would celebrate her seventh birthday. All the love Callie had kept bundled inside for her own child, she lavished on Nattie. Still, she clung to her secret. And until she had the courage to tell David and Grace, the secret was a barrier between them.

Without question, Nattie had wrought a change in her mother. Grace's critical martyrdom had faded, and in its place, she seemed to have found a joy in living. She would have made Callie's child a wonderful grandmother, after all.

No wedding had been mentioned, but Callie was sure marriage was David's intention. They had settled, without words, into a warm, committed relationship.

But marriage was built on honesty. She wanted to start the new year with the truth. And the longer she waited, the more difficult it would become. The last time she'd set a deadline for herself, she had sensed that God worked to bring it about sooner. Now, she set a second deadline. She would summon her courage, and by the first of January she would tell David about her baby.

Chapter Twenty-Two

Callie and Grace sat in the parlor, a fire glowing in the fireplace. Thanksgiving was still a week away, but the first snow had fallen early and muted the world outside. With David at work and Nattie in school, the house was also quiet.

Callie studied her mother, seated cozily in front of the fire reading a magazine. A year earlier, she would never have believed that her feelings for Grace would change so radically, but they had. And with a renewed fondness welling inside her, she knew the right moment had arrived.

"Mom, could we talk?"

Grace glanced up from the magazine, a look of tenderness etching her face. "I've been wanting to talk to you, too."

"You have?" For the first time in years, she saw her mother with clearer eyes. Grace had always loved her, but her love had seemed doled out in controlled portions, as if she were afraid she might give it all away at one time and have nothing left. Today she seemed different.

Grace tossed the magazine to the floor and leaned back in the chair. "I didn't want to come here at first. You knew that, of course. And I suppose you saw what changed my mind. That wonderful child. I can understand why you wanted to come back here, Callie, not only because of David, but for Nattie."

"I know. She stole my heart."

"And I think David has, as well. He's a loving man. Kind and generous. You couldn't find a better husband." She peered into Callie's eyes. "I pray that's what the two of you have in mind."

"I pray so, too, Mom. And I'm glad you like him."

"I do. But God gave both of us a gift in Nattie. I look at her, Callie, and all I can think is somewhere in this world there's another little girl just like her. Nattie's so much like you, Callie." Her lips trembled, and she paused, her voice hindered by emotion. "I can imagine what your own little girl is like right now."

Tears stung Callie's eyes. "That's what I want to talk about, Mom. Part is a confession—a terrible secret I kept from you for so many years. Part is to help you understand my hurt and anger toward you and Dad."

"What are you talking about?" Grace's face paled, her eyes narrowed.

"I kept things hidden from you, and I've done the same with David. He doesn't know that I had a child. But I'm going to tell him. He and Sara wanted a child so badly that they took life-threatening chances to have a baby. Sara couldn't continue her radiation or chemotherapy without harming the baby, and without it, she endangered her own life. How could I tell him I had one that I gave away?''

"Oh Callie, that was a whole different matter. You can't compare the two situations.''

"But I can. What would he think of me? I've worried that I'll disillusion him. He expects more of me. I always thought that you and Daddy felt that way, and I couldn't endure that rejection again from someone else I love so much.''

Grace threw her hand to her mouth, and her eyes brimmed with tears. "Not rejection, Callie. Your dad and I were so hurt for you. We were irritated that you protected the young man. That's the part that upset us. And naturally, we were disappointed.''

"And that's the part that hurt me so much, Mom.''

"We had such dreams for you—with all your talents and gifts from God. And your refusal to sing. We felt you were punishing us because we forced the adoption. But we always loved you and thought we were doing the right thing about the baby.''

"I know. And my anger at you wasn't fair. Because I never told you the whole story.''

Grace's body stiffened. "The whole story?''

"I couldn't tell you the truth, because I knew both of you would be crushed. And to be honest, I wondered if you'd believe me, because I felt guilty thinking I might be partly to blame for what happened.'' Pressure pushed against her chest and constricted her throat.

"Callie, you're talking in circles. Please, tell me what you mean. You're scaring me.''

Strangling on the words, Callie whispered, "The baby's father wasn't a college boy, Mother."

"Not a—" She faltered and clung to the chair. "Then, who?"

"I was raped." The word spilled out of her along with a torrent of blinding tears. Her body shook with the knotted, bitter hurt that had bound her for so many years. Telling David had been difficult, but telling her mother was devastating.

Grace rose with more speed than Callie could have imagined possible, and made her way to the sofa. She wrapped her arms around Callie and held her with every bit of strength she had. She asked no questions, but she held her daughter with the love only a mother could have for her child.

When Callie had regained control, she told Grace the story, in all its horror. Her mother listened, stroking and calming her until the awful truth was out. A ragged sigh raked through her shaking body.

Tears rolled down Grace's cheeks. No words were needed—Callie understood her mother's grief as well as she knew her own. They talked through the afternoon in a way they had never talked before. Their tears, like a cleansing flood, purified them, purged their past hurt and anger, and united them in love.

Ken joined them for Thanksgiving, and Grace had been content until then. But as Christmas approached, she urged Callie to take her home.

"Look how well I'm doing. My bedroom's upstairs now. I'm getting around. The cane is only a prop— see?" She lifted the cane and took a few steps. "I miss my house. And my things."

"That's why I don't have things, Mom. I've learned to live everywhere without a bunch of trappings."

"That's because all your trappings are with my things—at the house."

She chuckled at the truth. "I'll tell you what, Mom. Christmas is less than three weeks away. Why not stay here through the holidays, and then we'll take you home. You'll have nearly three weeks to get stronger."

"No sense in spending Christmas alone, is there?" David asked.

Grace eyed them both. "You promise? If I shut my mouth, you'll take me home after the holidays?"

"Promise," Callie said. "And think of what a nice Christmas you'll have this year with Nattie around. Christmas is always special with children."

Grace's face softened. "It has been a long time, hasn't it. You were my last baby."

David folded the paper and dropped it beside the chair. "And she's sure not a baby anymore." He winked at Grace.

"Me?" Nattie asked from the doorway, her brow puckered. "I'm not a baby anymore."

David opened his arms to her. "You sure aren't, Nat. But no, we were talking about Callie. She's no baby, either."

Nattie laughed. "I wish we had a baby."

Callie looked from Nattie to David, wondering what his response would be.

"First, we need a husband and wife. Then babies can come."

Nattie glanced at Callie. "You can marry Callie, Daddy. Then you'll be a husband and wife."

David gave her a giant hug. "My girl. She's making all the arrangements." His amused eyes sought Callie's. "We'll have to see about that, won't we?"

"Okay," Nattie said, and dropped the matter without another comment.

But Callie's heart pounded. Marriage seemed the next step for them, but the words were yet to be spoken. And Callie couldn't answer yes—not yet.

"I have an idea," Callie said.

Three pairs of eyes turned toward her. Surprise lit Grace's face. Callie grinned to herself—did Grace think Callie was about to propose? "Let's go out and buy a Christmas tree."

"Goody," Nattie said, jumping in place at David's side. Her enthusiasm was contagious.

"Before this child knocks me out with her exuberance, I suppose we ought to do just that. A Christmas tree, it is," David said.

For Callie, many years had passed since she'd decorated a house. But this year, she joined in the excitement. The tree stood in the family parlor, covered in lights and bulbs. The house smelled of ginger and vanilla, and every day Callie and Nattie tiptoed into the kitchen to snatch a cookie or two from Agnes's baking.

Four days before Christmas, to Callie's dismay, David had to squeeze in a two-day business trip, returning Christmas Eve.

With David's absence, Callie felt lonely. The house was silent, and she opened her door and glanced across the hallway. Nattie seemed too quiet, and she wondered if the child missed David, too, or if something else bothered her.

She tiptoed across the hall and peeked through the doorway. Nattie was curled on bed with a book on her lap. She looked up when Callie came into the room.

"So, how are you doing?" Callie asked, sitting on the edge of her bed.

"Okay."

"Just okay? And with Christmas coming so soon? I thought you'd be all excited."

She looked at Nattie's face and saw a question in her eyes. "Is something wrong, Nat?"

Nattie snuggled down into her bed, turning her head on the pillow. "If you marry my daddy, would you have a baby?"

Callie's pulse skipped a beat. "Only God can answer that, Nattie. Would you like a new baby?"

She nodded yet her eyes blinked as if a fearful thought hung in her mind.

"What are you worried about, sweetie?" Did she wonder if Callie and David had enough love to share?

Nattie lowered her eyelids. "Would you die if you had a baby?"

A ragged sigh shivered through Callie, and she slid her legs onto the bed and curled up next to Nattie. "No, Nattie, I wouldn't die. Are you thinking of your mom?"

Her head moved against the pillow, nodding. "When my mommy was sick, Daddy said he was sorry that I was born, because it made Mommy die."

Callie struggled to contain her gasp. "Oh, Nattie,

your daddy wouldn't say that. He loves you so much. Your parents wanted you so badly, and Miriam said that you gave your mom and dad so much happiness. No, no, you couldn't have heard your daddy say that. Maybe you misunderstood.''

"Because my mommy was having a baby, she couldn't get her medicine, and she died. So I made her die, didn't I?''

"Is that what's made you sad all this time, Nattie?''

Nattie didn't have to speak. Her face reflected the answer. Callie understood now—Nattie's silence for so long, her burden of guilt that she had caused her mother's death.

She wrapped Nattie in her arms and held her tightly against her chest. Looking at the little girl's blue eyes, nearly the color of her own, she knew this would be what she'd feel for her own child. She couldn't love her own flesh any more than she had grown to love Nattie. And Nattie's hurt was her own.

"Whatever you heard, Nattie, I think, you didn't understand. Your mom had a bad disease for a long time. God was so good to her and gave her four years to spend with you before she went to heaven. Do you remember how much she loved you?''

"Uh-huh,'' Nattie whispered. "She hugged me like you do.'' Her small arms wound more tightly around Callie's neck. "Callie?'' Her voice was a whisper.

"What, sweetheart?''

"Could you be my mommy?''

"I think I am already, Nattie. I love you as if you were my own daughter. I couldn't love you more.'' The words caught in her throat. "And your daddy thinks you're the greatest in the whole wide world. So does Grandma Grace.''

Nattie nodded. ''Grandma loves me. She told me.''

''She did, huh? You go to sleep. Your daddy'll be home tomorrow.'' She nestled Nattie in her arms, singing softly in her ear.

What could Nattie have heard? When David returned, Callie would know.

Chapter Twenty-Three

David stepped into the foyer loaded with packages, and Callie rushed into his arms, suppressing her questions. He lowered the bags, and, despite the snow that clung to his coat, he pulled her to him and pressed his icy lips against her warm, eager mouth. "What a greeting. I should go away more often."

"Don't you dare." She dodged from his damp, chilled arms.

"So where's my favorite daughter?"

He heard a giggle, and Nattie leaped through the parlor doorway into his arms and planted a loud kiss on his cheek.

"You're freezing, Daddy."

"And your snuggly warm, Nattie."

She wiggled until he released her.

David slid off his coat, and Callie took it from him as he retrieved his packages.

"What have you got there?" she asked, eyeing the parcels.

"Wouldn't *you* like to know?"

"Yes, I would."

"Me, too," Nattie added. "Did you buy me a present?"

"Both of you are nosy. Yes, they're all Christmas surprises, so you'll have to wait. And before I let you two bury your noses in the bags, I'm taking them upstairs right now."

Callie and Nattie pretended to pout, but David ignored them and scooted up the stairs, carrying the bulging shopping bags.

He tossed them into his closet, then changed into his khaki slacks and a rust-and-green pullover. Before closing the door, he glanced with an anxious grin at the packages.

While in Bloomington, he had wandered through a jewelry store, finally selecting a gold locket for Nattie as delicate and lovely as she was.

His heart tripped when he thought of Callie's gift. As well as a gold chain with pearl and garnet beads, David had selected an engagement ring. Christmas Day, he would propose.

After he dressed, David returned to the first floor, admiring the holiday decor. For two years his Christmas spirit had lain dormant. Today, with Callie at his side, he felt complete.

As he neared the bottom of the stairs, Callie beckoned him through the library door, a strange look on her face.

"Something wrong?"

"Push the door closed, would you?" she asked. "I want to make sure we're alone before we talk."

Feeling his pulse quicken, he gave the door a push.

Her face told him she was terribly concerned. "What is it?"

"Something happened while you were gone, and I've been anxious to talk to you." She glanced over her shoulder at a chair. "Let's sit, okay?"

"Sure," he said, folding his tense body into a nearby recliner. "I see you're upset."

"It's something Nattie said. I think I know what's been bothering her all this time."

His pulse throbbed in his temples. "What is it?"

Callie blurted her story. Confusion and worry tangled in her words, and as he listened, he forced his mind back nearly three years, trying to decipher what Nattie might have heard.

"Callie, I don't know. I can't imagine what she heard. We never talked in front of her. Sara and I were very open about her illness and about her ill-fated pregnancy, but not with Nattie around. I was so angry and guilty when Sara had the miscarriage. But that was a year before Natalie—"

"Could she have overheard you talking when Sara was...really bad. Near the end?"

"If Nattie was listening, I didn't know. Yes, I was terribly upset. I knew Sara's pregnancy was a mistake. Stopping her treatment risked her life, and then we lost the baby, anyway. Oh, Callie, I probably yelled at her, telling her how foolish we were to try and have a child. I was a maniac right before she died."

"If Nattie heard it, she blamed herself."

"But she wasn't to blame. And Nattie should know that. She couldn't have been to blame."

Callie's eyes questioned him, her forehead furrowing in confusion. "Why, David? Sara couldn't have treatment during either pregnancy. Why *wouldn't* Nattie feel to blame?"

David's world crumbled around him. Words he hadn't said since Sara died rose to his lips. Nattie had been told, but she had been young. Maybe she'd forgotten. They had to raise her to know the truth.

"Answer me, David. Why?"

He struggled to say the words. "When Sara lost the baby, we knew that was our last chance. Nattie isn't my biological child, Callie. She was adopted."

Callie stopped as if struck by a sniper's bullet. Blood drained from her face. Trembling uncontrollably, she raised her hand to her chest. "Adopted?" She rose, her legs quaking. "Adopted?" she whispered. "And you never told me."

"Oh Callie, to me, Nattie was our own. I rarely think about—" He stopped speaking. Callie had dashed from the room and up the stairs.

Weakness overcame her. Callie stood in her room, holding her face in her hands, disbelieving. Why had David lied to her? But…he hadn't lied. He hadn't told her, that was all. A wave of sorrow washed over her. Neither had she told *him* the whole truth.

Adoption. Had David not spoken of it for a reason? Was he ashamed? Her chest tightened, restricting her breathing. She closed her bedroom door and locked it, then threw herself across the bed. Callie's own sorrow tore through her. *Nattie.* This beautiful child, like her own daughter, had been signed away—placed in someone else's home. And somewhere, another mother wondered about *her* lost child. The paradox knifed her. *Why Lord? Why should mothers feel such pain?*

She needed to calm down and reason. Callie closed her eyes, whispering a long-needed prayer to God. Compassion, wisdom, understanding. She needed so much. Yet, so often she wore herself out trying to solve every problem on her own. God had guided her to this house. Was this His purpose?

She loved Nattie as her own, and the child almost could be hers: they had the same coloring and talents. But she knew in her heart, Nattie wasn't. She belonged to someone else.

She curled on her side and prayed aloud. *"Lord, please help me to understand. You tell us to seek You and You'll hear us. With all my heart Lord, I need to find peace and comfort. I want to understand."*

A light rap sounded on the door. *David.* She ignored his knock and his hushed voice, calling her name. For now, she had to think on her own. She could apologize for her behavior and explain her strange reaction later.

Finally, she rose and washed her face, staring at the pale image in the mirror that gaped back at her. Tonight was Christmas Eve, and Ken would arrive soon. This was not the moment for confessions and confusion. Now she needed to look presentable.

She retouched her makeup and tossed a teal-blue dress over her head, cinching the belt around her waist. The rosebud brooch from David lay on her dresser, and she pinned it to her shoulder. *Better? Yes, look better.* She unlocked the door and descended the stairs.

Ken had already arrived, and called to her from the bottom landing. "Merry Christmas, Callie."

"Merry Christmas, Ken," she echoed.

David watched from behind her brother. Though handsome in his navy suit, tension ridged David's face, and he looked less than merry. She gave her brother a kiss on the cheek, then spoke to David. "I see you're ready for church."

"Yes. You look lovely, Callie." He gave her brother a friendly pat on the shoulder. "Go ahead, Ken. Let's sit in the parlor with the Christmas tree."

Ken went ahead, joining Nattie and Grace, and David leaned close to her ear as they followed him. "We need to talk."

"Later, David, please. I owe you an explanation."

He nodded, but she felt his arm tense. Tenderly, she pressed his forearm, hoping he understood and forgave her. A faint movement flickered at the corner of his mouth, and she relaxed, believing that he did understand.

With conversations flowing in many directions, the time passed, and Agnes soon announced their early dinner. The children's Christmas program began at seven-thirty, and Nattie had to arrive by seven.

At the church, they sat near the front. Beginning with "Oh, Come Little Children," the youngsters proceeded down the aisle, dressed as shepherds, wise men, Mary, Joseph and the angels.

Nattie's halo bounced as she marched past the rows in her white flowing robe and sparkling angel wings. When she saw the family, she raised her hand in a tiny wave.

The children took their places, and families beamed

as the little actors spoke with practiced precision. When the angels chorused, "Peace on earth; goodwill to men," Nattie's voice rose above the rest, every word clear and distinct.

At the end of the program, they descended the stairs to the Sunday School rooms, while the children stripped off their costumes.

Nattie dashed to them when they hit the landing. "Was I good? I knew all my lines."

David crouched down and gave her a hug. "We were all very proud of you."

Callie's heart twisted, watching him with Nattie. So much love and devotion for his daughter. Natural or adopted, she was his child.

When David retreated to locate Nattie's coat, a familiar voice sailed toward Callie.

"Well, Merry Christmas."

Turning, Callie cranked her facial muscles into a smile. "Hello, Mary Beth. Merry Christmas."

A man was attached to her arm, and she batted her eyes toward her escort. "Callie, do you know Charles Robinson?"

"Not formally, but I know you from church. It's nice to meet you. And this is my brother, Ken." They shook hands. Saving further conversation, David returned just then with Nattie, now buttoned into her coat. After final amenities, they headed toward the door.

Once home, as they entered the foyer, the parlor clock chimed ten, and eager for Christmas Day, Nattie headed for bed with David's promise to tuck her in. Callie longed to talk with David but she had to join the others for Agnes's homemade cookies and coffee.

The conversation flowed until Callie yawned, followed by David. Finally, they agreed it was time to turn in.

David rose first. "I'd better call it a night. I still have a few 'Santa' things to do for tomorrow morning."

Ken followed and helped Grace up the stairs. As they made their way, Callie turned to David. "Can we talk now?"

He hesitated. "Let me get this stuff set up, so I won't feel hurried. I'll knock on your door when I'm finished."

Disappointment needled her, but he was right. They didn't need to be rushed. Their talk would be important, and she wanted to be emotionally ready. "Okay. I'll be waiting."

Upstairs, Callie paused outside Nattie's room. In the glow of the pink night-light, the child lay in a soft flush of color. Callie stood over her, her hand stroking the golden curls fanned out on the pillow. Nattie slept soundly.

Callie leaned over, brushing Nattie's cheek with her lips, then whispered, "I love you, Nattie." Her heart stirred with loving awareness. It didn't matter whose child she was—Nattie was loved and cherished. God had guided the baby to this house and to a Christian family who loved her.

Brushing the tears from her cheeks, Callie crossed the hall and slipped into a caftan, then waited. Her nerves pitched at each creak of the house, wondering if it was David. Tonight she would tell him about her daughter. How would he feel? And how did she feel? *Peace and understanding, Lord.* Her prayer lifted again. She pushed her door ajar and moved her chair so she could see David approach.

When he appeared, he passed her room and crossed to Nattie's. Surprised, Callie rose, padding softly to the doorway, but he only peeked in and then turned.

"You're waiting. I'm sorry it took so long. You know how it is assembling toys."

A knot tightened in her stomach. No, she didn't know.

"Let's sit," David said, drawing the desk chair beside her recliner. "We have lots to talk about."

Callie sank into the cushion. "I'm sorry, David. I was shocked. I—"

"First, let me explain, please. I wasn't hiding Nattie's adoption. When you first came, the thought entered my mind. But I didn't know you and wanted you to treat her as my own. Then, you grew to love her as I do, and the thought faded. She is my daughter. I love her no differently than I would a natural child."

"Please, David. My shock is more complex than you can imagine. Yes, I was startled when you told me. And then I wondered if you were ashamed of her adoption, and—"

"Ashamed? How could I be? Sara and I chose her. She was ours from her first days on earth. We nurtured her, loved her, cared for her. How could I be ashamed? I thank God for my beautiful daughter, Callie."

Her tears flowed, dripping to her hands knotted in her lap. She raised them to cover her face.

David rose and knelt at her feet. "Don't cry. Please. I don't understand what's happened."

"David, I didn't know how I was going to tell you this. I was so worried you'd hate me or wonder what kind of person I am."

David pulled her hands from her face. "Whatever it is, just tell me." He held her hands captive in his.

She closed her eyes, tears dripping from her chin. "After I was raped, I found out I was pregnant."

"Pregnant—oh, Callie, my love." Tears rimmed his eyes.

"My parents thought the father was a college boy, and I let them believe it. I had a baby girl, David, born on Christmas Day. I placed her up for adoption."

"My love, how could I hate you? You were blameless. And hurt far more than I ever knew."

"But you did so much to have a baby—taking horrible chances. And I didn't fight to keep my child. I haven't forgiven myself. Every day I ask God why it happened—and if she's okay. Is she happy? Do her parents love her?"

David rose, lifted her from the chair, and cradled her in his arms. "Oh, my dear, look around you. Look at the beautiful child that gave Sara and me such joy. Wouldn't God do the same for your child? Trust in the Lord, Callie. You have strong faith in so many things. Believe that God placed your daughter in a home as filled with love as this one."

"I want to believe that." Music stirred in Callie's mind. She paused. The sad song that played within her heart faded, and a new melody filled her—a sense of peace and understanding. And love. "I went to Nattie's room when I came up and looked at her sweet face." The music lifted at the memory. "I couldn't love my own child more, David. I almost feel as if God has given me another chance."

"He has, my love, He has. And He's given us another chance. You've brought such joy to our lives. Nattie and I were shadows when you came, but you breathed new life into us—just as you gave life to your little daughter years ago."

The grandfather clock in the parlor began to chime. *One. Two. Three...* They paused, listening for the last. "It's midnight. Christmas Day." She didn't say what else lay in her heart. His eyes told her he knew.

"Doubt is part of life, Callie. When we first brought Nattie home, I wondered if I could love her. *Really* love her—like a true father. And—"

"You don't have to say it. If anyone was ever a true and loving father, it's you."

"And if anyone was ever a true and loving mother, it's you."

Callie looked into his face, and saw love glowing in his eyes. Her heart felt as if it would burst, and joy danced through her body. "A mother. It's a beautiful thought."

"A mother." Trance-like, David repeated her words and kissed her hair. He tilted her chin upward until their eyes met. "Callie, this is perfect. I planned this for tomorrow, but wait. Wait. Don't move."

He darted from the room, and in a moment returned to drop to his knees in front of her for the second time that night. "I've loved you for so long. You've brought happiness and completeness into our empty world, and, praise God, you've given me a healthy daughter. Nattie loves you so much and so do I. We would like to marry you, Callie. Will you be my wife? And Nattie's mother?"

Tears rolled down his cheeks as he handed her the blue velvet box. Callie knew what was inside, and without hesitating, she whispered her answer. "You know, I love you both with all my heart. Please forgive me for my foolish doubts and fears. I'm so filled with happiness—"

"And?"

She looked into his loving eyes. "And yes, I'll marry you."

His face brightened; the tension melted away. "Open the box, Callie." He turned it in her hand to face her.

She lifted the lid. Inside, a roping of three shades of gold entwined three sparkling diamonds. She raised her eyes. "Three shades of gold. And three diamonds. One for each of us."

"One for each of us. And we can always add a fourth."

His eyes glowed, and with quivering fingers, he took the ring from her and slipped it on her finger. "Perfect." His gaze caressed her face. "Yes, perfect."

She opened her mouth to speak, but he quieted her with his warm, tender lips. Captured in his arms, Callie's fears and shame were gone. Her black dreams could hurt no more. She nestled securely against David's chest, finally whole and at peace.

When their lips parted, they tiptoed, hand in hand, across the hall to gaze at their beautiful child, sleeping peacefully in a rosy glow of light.

Epilogue

On Christmas Day, a month before Nattie's ninth birthday, the family gathered in church. Even Callie's sister, Patricia, and her husband had come from California for the holiday. They arrived, eager to see Randolph David Hamilton, who'd been born in early November.

Grace held the baby in her arms, with Nattie nestled as close as she could without sitting on Grace's lap.

David and Callie stood at the front, their faces glowing with wide, proud grins. David's gaze drifted with admiration to his wife, almost as trim again as she had been before her nine months of "ballooning," as they'd called it. He couldn't take his eyes from her.

"What?" Callie whispered. "Why are you staring at me?"

"Because you're beautiful, and I'm the happiest

man alive." He squeezed her arm and tilted his head toward the children, sitting in the third pew.

She teased him with the nudge of her hip. "Well, you'd better focus on the music. We have to sing in a minute."

The organ music voluntary ended, and the ushers brought the offering plates to the front. As they retreated down the aisle, the organist played the introductory notes to the duet.

The opening strains began, and Callie's mind soared back to a Christmas midnight two years earlier—to the moment her past vanished and God's purpose became clear. On that day, a new life began.

Her gaze drifted to Nattie, growing lovelier each day, now looking at her with pure, joyous love. Somewhere on this Christmas night, another young girl celebrated Jesus's birth and her own birthday. Assurance filled Callie, as she trusted that God had guided her own baby daughter to a loving, Christian family.

Callie wiped away an invading tear. Today, with happiness, she looked at her son, the image of his handsome father. Raising her eyes to David's, she felt complete and wonderful. His smile captivated her, and she sighed.

As the last note of the introduction sounded, they each drew in a deep breath, then lifted their voices in the familiar words of an old carol that now rang with new meaning. *"It came upon a midnight clear, that glorious song of old...."*

* * * * *

Dear Reader,

Sometimes a story weaves through a writer's mind, and when hands touch the keyboard, the story writes itself. This was my experience with *Upon a Midnight Clear*. Though I have never lost a child through death or adoption, I have experienced both of those deep hurts through family and friends. At times like this, sorrow can take over a happy heart and create secrets that wound the spirit.

Many of us cling to our deepest fears, sorrows and sins because we do not trust. Yet love can heal the worst transgression, making us whole again, just as our Savior has washed us clean and made us snow-white with His forgiveness.

I hope you've enjoyed Callie, David and Nattie's story. Their experience offers comfort and hope to us all. Don't suffer alone. Sharing pain and hurt with others draws us closer together and heals our secret wounds. And talk to the Lord. We can experience God's undying love by asking forgiveness and accepting His grace.

Gail Gaymer Martin